ROYAL HOLIDAY

Royal Holiday

JASMINE GUILLORY

BERKLEY
NEW YORK

BERKLEY
An imprint of Penguin Random House LLC
penguinrandomhouse.com

Copyright © 2019 by Jasmine Guillory
Penguin Random House supports copyright. Copyright fuels creativity, encourages
diverse voices, promotes free speech, and creates a vibrant culture. Thank you for buying
an authorized edition of this book and for complying with copyright laws by not
reproducing, scanning, or distributing any part of it in any form without permission.
You are supporting writers and allowing Penguin Random House to continue
to publish books for every reader.

BERKLEY and the BERKLEY & B colophon are registered trademarks of Penguin
Random House LLC.

Library of Congress Cataloging-in-Publication Data

Names: Guillory, Jasmine, author.
Title: Royal holiday / Jasmine Guillory.
Description: First edition. | New York: Berkley, 2019.
Identifiers: LCCN 2019024644 (print) | LCCN 2019024645 (ebook) |
ISBN 9781984802217 (hardcover) | ISBN 9781984802224 (ebook)
Subjects: LCSH: Dating (Social customs)—Fiction. | Romance fiction.
Classification: LCC PS3607.U48553 R69 2019 (print) |
LCC PS3607.U48553 (ebook) | DDC 813/.6—dc23
LC record available at https://lccn.loc.gov/2019024644
LC ebook record available at https://lccn.loc.gov/2019024645

First Edition: October 2019

Printed in the United States of America
1   3   5   7   9   10   8   6   4   2

Cover art and design by Vikki Chu
Book design by Kristin del Rosario

To my grandmother,
Joyce York-Brown.
Thank you for everything.

Acknowledgments

Every book only comes to be because of hard work and help from many people, and that's especially the case for this book.

I'm so grateful for my incredible agent, Holly Root, and my fantastic editor, Cindy Hwang, for their enthusiasm and support when I came to them with this idea. I'm thrilled and relieved every day that I'm going through this publishing journey with the two of you to guide me.

To everyone at Berkley, thank you for your hard work, energy, and ambition for me and my books, especially Jessica Brock, Fareeda Bullert, Angela Kim, Craig Burke, Erin Galloway, Kristine Swartz, Jin Yu, Megha Jain, and Vikki Chu. Thank you to Lauren Monaco, Jen Trzaska, and everyone on the incredible Penguin Random House sales team. And huge thanks to Kate Byrne and the entire Headline Eternal team for their guidance and enthusiasm.

I could never have done any of this without all the encouragement, support, and advice I've gotten from so many other writers. Amy Spalding and Akilah Brown, you've been there for me since the very beginning; I owe so much to both of you. Ruby Lang, thank you for everything. Heather Cocks and Jessica Morgan, you are two of the most delightful, inspiring, and helpful writers out there, and I've learned so much from both of you. Sarah Mackey, thank you so much for both your enthusiastic cheerleading and your American to British translations. Lauren Kiehna, thank you for the incredible website TheCourtJeweller.com—it's helped me more than you can know. Jami Attenberg, Melissa Baumgart, Robin Benway, Austin Channing Brown, Kayla Cagan, Alexis Coe, Nicole Chung, Roxane Gay, Tayari Jones, Lyz Lenz, Caille Millner, Daniel Ortberg, Doree Shafrir, Kate Spencer, Laura Turner, Esmé Weijun Wang, Sarah Weinman, and Sara Zarr, I am so grateful to have you all in my life.

Thank you so much to all of my friends who put up with me when I fell off the face of the earth to write this book, especially Jill Vizas, Nicole Clouse, Simi Patnaik, Janet Goode, Melissa Sladden, Jina Kim, Lisa McIntire, Ryan Gallagher, Sarah Tiedeman, Kyle Wong, Julian Davis Mortenson, Nanita Cranford, Joy Alferness, Alicia Harris, Toby Rugger, Rachel Fershleiser, Maret Orliss, Maggie Levine, Sara Kate Wilkinson, Kate Leos, and Lyette Mercier. And special thanks to Lindsey Kistler for literally putting me up in London while I did research, and for all of our discussions about the U.K. and the U.S.—this book is better because of you.

To my family, especially my parents and my sister, I love you so much. Thank you for always being in my corner and by my side.

Nicole Cliffe and Samantha Powell, our royals group chat has brought me so much joy in the past few years, and I'm not sure this book would have happened without the two of you.

Thanks to Meghan and Harry, just because.

And finally, Margaret H. Willison: You're the real MVP. Thank you for giving me the idea for this book, for your all-caps enthusiasm when you found out I was actually going to write it, and for being the incredible person you are.

Chapter One

Vivian nudged her daughter as they walked out of the customs area at Heathrow Airport.

"Um, Maddie? Do you think Ms. M. Forest and Ms. V. Forest are us?"

Vivian gestured at the man in the suit, holding the sign with their names on it.

Maddie turned in the direction Vivian was looking and grinned at her mother.

"Let's do this, Mom."

Vivian looked around and laughed to herself before she grinned back at Maddie.

She still didn't exactly know how she'd gotten here. It had all started with a call from Maddie a few weeks ago.

"Hey, Mom, I need an answer fast—do you want to spend Christmas with me in England?"

Vivian had laughed. What else was there to do when your thirty-four-year-old daughter asked something so ridiculous?

"Sure, I do. I also want to spend Thanksgiving with you in Hawaii, New Year's Eve with you in Paris, and Easter with you in Rome."

But Maddie didn't laugh at that.

"No, really. I'm serious. You remember my old mentor, Amelia Samuels?"

Vivian looked away from her computer screen.

"The one who's now the stylist for the princess?"

"Duchess, but yes. Well, Amelia was supposed to go to England at Christmas to help prepare the Duchess for all of the royal Christmas festivities—apparently, there are lots of them—but Amelia is pregnant with twins and just had to go on bed rest. Her doctor says she's under too much stress and can't work at all."

"Oh no, really? Poor Amelia; I didn't know she was pregnant! Please tell her I'm thinking about her."

Vivian had only met Amelia once, that time she'd gone down to visit Maddie when she'd been living in L.A., but she'd really liked her. And Amelia had done a lot for Maddie and her own stylist career.

"I will, Mom, but let me finish. Since Amelia can't fly to England for Christmas, she wants me to fill in for her, because both she and the Duchess want someone she trusts."

Vivian dropped her pen on the floor.

"Maddie! Oh my God! Are you serious? My daughter is going to be so famous! You're going to England to work with a princess? You'll be all over *People* magazine! Oh my God, I can't wait to tell everybody!"

Maddie laughed.

"You can't tell everybody yet, but I know, I'm blown away. But wait, we can be excited in a second—I want you to come with me."

Vivian got up and closed her office door.

"Come with you . . . to England?"

Maddie started talking faster.

"It means I'll be there for Christmas, and I don't want to be alone with a bunch of strangers at Christmas. I already asked if you could join me, and they said yes. So . . . can you?"

Vivian looked around at the piles of work on her desk, and in the direction of her boss's office, with their last conversation about his future—and hers—ringing in her ears.

"Maddie, I don't know about this—I have a ton of work at this time of year, and today is especially wild around here. What about Theo, did you already talk to him?"

Vivian already adored Maddie's boyfriend, Theo, even though they'd only officially been together for a few months.

"I told Theo about the offer, yes, and he's thrilled for me. But if you mean did I invite Theo to come to England with me already, absolutely not. I love Theo, and I can't wait to spend New Year's Eve with him, but I've never spent a Christmas without my mother, and I don't intend to start now. So, are you coming?"

Vivian grinned to herself. She couldn't deny it warmed her heart to know her daughter still wanted her mom with her for Christmas.

But to go all the way to England for Christmas? That far away from work, the rest of the family, and everything?

"I'd love to come, but I can't make a decision like this right now," she said to Maddie. "Let me think about it and we can talk about this in a few days."

Maddie's voice got louder.

"There's no 'a few days.' I have to make this decision now, and I'm going to decide for both of us. You need this. You haven't gone on a real vacation in years."

How had she managed to have a daughter who thought she could boss her around like this?

"Oh, *you* have to go. Life is too short not to take incredible opportunities like this! But I don't think I can—"

"I'm definitely going, and you're definitely coming with me. You never take enough time for yourself; you know I always tell you that. You spend all your time working or helping me or helping out with Aunt Jo. I know you don't want to leave Aunt Jo, but you need a break."

"Maddie . . ."

"Great, it's settled. Talk to you later!"

And with that, Maddie had hung up, and two days later they had plane tickets. Vivian hadn't even known until they were about to board the flight that they were first-class tickets.

She laughed to herself just thinking about that flight. The last time she'd been on an airplane, she'd felt lucky to be in an aisle seat. She'd had an aisle seat this time, too—a huge, futuristic, podlike seat, with room not only to stretch her legs, but to lie almost flat. With just a wave, she could summon champagne and snacks to her side, and for all she knew, there was some secret button to give her a massage, too. She and Maddie had spent the first two hours of the flight just looking around and giggling with each other.

Despite how amazing the flight had been, Vivian still wasn't sure she should be here. She was with Maddie, but what about the rest of her family? Her sisters needed her, especially her sister Jo. And she'd never been away from the Bay Area for Christmas in her life. What was Christmas going to be like without her great-aunt Shirley's ham, or her cousin Loretta's greens, or those dinner rolls her cousin Marilyn always said she made but everyone else knew she got at Safeway?

But then . . . she hated those greens. There was never enough pork in them and way too much vinegar. It might be nice to have a change of pace for Christmas, even though she had serious doubts anyone in England knew how to make a sweet potato pie.

The very polite man in the suit escorted them to a waiting SUV, and Vivian and Maddie kept making faces at each other as he offered them three different kinds of bottled water and told them how to turn on their heated seats.

Maddie opened a bottle of water and handed it to Vivian.

"It's supposed to take a few hours to get there, so . . ."

"What?" Vivian stopped her. "A few hours? Where are we going?"

Maddie laughed.

"Didn't you read the email I sent you about that? The royal family always spends Christmas at Sandringham. It's up in the north of England."

Like she'd had time to read Maddie's lengthy emails. She'd gotten herself packed and to the airport, hadn't she?

"I had too much to do in the last few weeks; I had to get ready for a last-minute international trip, remember? Plus, your emails are too long."

Maddie sighed.

"I should have known. Anyway, Sandringham is a big estate; there are a bunch of royal residences on it, and then lots of trees and land; at least, that's what the pictures online look like. I guess we'll see for ourselves shortly."

Vivian sat back against the plush heated seat.

"I still can't believe we're really staying with the Duke and Duchess."

Maddie had told her this for the first time about a week ago, and like everything else Maddie had told her about this trip, it sounded as though it couldn't be real.

Maddie shook her head.

"I know. The Duchess insisted. She said it would be easier if I was right on-site, and that there's plenty of room in their cottage on the estate for us. When she was so enthusiastic about you joining me, I suspected she was missing her own mom, so I think she's really looking forward to having us there."

This all seemed surreal. Vivian really couldn't believe she was about to meet someone she'd read so much about.

She was a social worker from Oakland, for God's sake! How was this happening?

Speaking of her job . . .

"So, I haven't told you this yet," Vivian said to her daughter, "because I wasn't sure if it was really going to happen, but Darren made the announcement before I left the office yesterday: he's retiring. And he wants me to get his job. He first talked to me about it a few weeks ago, and yesterday he brought it up to his boss when I was right there, so I guess he means it."

Maddie screeched.

"Mom! Oh my God! I can't believe you're just telling me this now! This is so exciting! What's the title, director of social work?"

Vivian nodded slowly.

"Yep. He's leaving sometime in February, and the hospital director already told me they probably won't get the hiring process started for a few months, so they're going to make me the acting director as soon as Darren retires."

"Wow." Maddie put her water bottle down and pulled her mom into a hug. "I'm so thrilled for you; this is such great recognition after all of your hard work."

The recognition had felt satisfying, even though she was still in shock about all of this.

"That's true, though it means I'll be jumping into a job with lots of hard work, and I won't get to see patients nearly as much . . . or maybe not at all. But it's a big honor"—she grinned—"and more money."

Maddie settled back against the car seat.

"Well, I'm even more glad I made you come on this trip

with me. I'm sure you'll take even fewer vacations once you're the big boss."

That was probably very true. Yes, she was glad she'd come on this trip with her daughter. She hadn't been on vacation—a real vacation, not just a few days off work—in a year and a half. The only other time she'd even been out of the country was that trip she'd taken with her friends to Mexico for her fortieth birthday, and that had been well over ten years ago.

She looked out the car window for her first glimpses of England. The sun was setting already, which surprised her, since they'd landed in the middle of the afternoon. She reminded herself how much farther north London was from the Bay Area, and it was almost the shortest day of the year; of course sunset was this early.

After about an hour and a half, the car slowed down. She and Maddie peered out the windows into the darkness—they couldn't see much, but it seemed like they were turning off the highway and onto smaller roads. Then the car slowed down even more, and it got darker outside the car windows; the streetlights had seemed to disappear, and all she could see were the outlines of trees. She and Maddie looked at each other with their eyes wide open.

Vivian reached out and grabbed her daughter's hand and squeezed hard.

"You're going to be great at this."

Maddie nodded.

"Thanks, Mom. I'm so glad you're here."

Vivian smiled.

"Me too."

Just then, the car came to a stop, and the very polite driver leaped out of his seat to open their car doors.

"Madam. Madam. Welcome to Sandringham."

Vivian turned to Maddie.

"Deep breaths," she said under her voice, before she turned to get out of the car.

"Thank you," Vivian said to the driver. She reached for her carry-on, but before she could pick it up, someone else had come running.

"Allow me, ma'am."

With nothing to carry, she and Maddie turned toward the . . . cottage? Was this a cottage? Oh God. She would have called it a mansion, but then, they did have different words for things in England. She still couldn't remember what they called a bathroom. She was going to have to ask Maddie.

They walked up to the front door, but before they got to the top step, yet another man in a suit opened it.

"Ms. Forest and Ms. Forest? Welcome."

Vivian and Maddie turned to each other and smiled before walking inside.

They'd just taken their coats off and handed them to Suit #3, when a woman came down the hall toward them.

"You're here! I'm so glad you made it! How was your flight? Was the drive here okay? I know it's so cold outside, but we've made up the fires in your rooms. Would you like a hot buttered rum to warm you up after your trip? Some sandwiches or scones, maybe?"

She was smaller in person, but even prettier than she looked on the cover of *People* magazine. Vivian hoped Maddie would get to find out exactly what her skin care regimen was, because the woman was glowing.

Vivian reached out her hand.

"Thank you so much, and thank you for your hospitality. Both the flight and the drive were very easy. And I can't speak for my daughter, but hot buttered rum sounds like a dream come true."

Maddie laughed.

"And so do sandwiches and scones."

The Duchess ignored Vivian's hand and pulled her into a hug instead.

"Wonderful! Let me take you upstairs, show you to your rooms, and let you get freshened up, then you can come down to the sitting room for a little feast. Don't worry; I'm sure you're exhausted. I don't want to keep you up too late. I know how those flights from California to England can be!"

The Duchess led them up two flights of stairs, chattering the entire time. Vivian hadn't expected her to be so normal. She'd worried that everything here would be super formal, and she'd have to be on her best behavior for her whole vacation, but the past five minutes had reassured her.

The Duchess threw open the doors of two rooms.

"Here are your rooms, and the bathroom is right across the hall." Vivian looked inside; their bags were already in their respective rooms.

And each room really had a fireplace, with a blazing fire. Bedrooms with fireplaces—she was never going to get over this.

"The house can get really drafty; that's why I had them make up the fires in there for you. I would have put space heaters in all of the rooms, but I made that mistake early on and blew out the electricity for about half of the palace, and everyone is still talking about it, so I've had to go back to things like fires and lots of throw rugs and hot tea. Just preparing you now so you won't wake up overnight shivering."

Sure enough, the next morning, Vivian woke up, huddled deep down under the many blankets piled on the bed. The night before, in the warm and toasty room, she'd thought there were way too many blankets on the bed—she'd counted at least five, one of which was a heavy wool blanket folded at the foot. But at some point overnight, the fire had gone out, and she'd managed to pull every single blanket over herself.

She had no idea what time it was, but light from the window was coming into the room, so it must be morning. She forced herself out of bed, even though she knew she could happily sleep for at least a few more hours—she hadn't fallen asleep until pretty late the night before, either because of jet lag, or excitement, she wasn't sure which. But she was only going to be in England for a handful of days; she didn't want to waste any of the daylight. Especially since they didn't appear to have a ton of it.

She checked her phone to see if anyone at home had

texted, but no, it was the middle of the night there, wasn't it? She sent a quick text to her sister Jo to see how she was feeling. Jo's cancer had been in remission this time for six months, and while she was a lot better, she was still pretty weak. Vivian had felt really guilty about leaving her, but Jo had laughed at her and told her there was no way she should miss this trip.

Vivian walked across the hall to the bathroom and wondered what she was going to do all day. Maddie would be working, and Vivian wasn't quite sure how much she was allowed to just wander around a royal estate on her own. Come to think of it, she wasn't sure about how a lot of things would operate for the next few days—for instance, how was she going to manage to get coffee this morning? This wasn't some bed-and-breakfast where there would be coffee and tea and muffins down in the living room. And her lack of sleep the night before meant she needed that coffee.

No matter what, she'd better go downstairs showered, with her hair in place, and with a bra on. There might be a prince in the kitchen, for God's sake.

When she walked back into her room after her shower (first scanning the hallway to make sure no royalty was around to see her in a towel), she noticed a piece of paper on the floor by the door.

Morning, Mom! I'll be closeted away (no pun intended) all morning making clothes decisions and doing fittings, but I've been instructed to tell you to head into the kitchen whenever you wake up and decide you want breakfast.—Maddie

Okay, so she was supposed to just head into the kitchen, presumably to find whoever made the amazing sandwiches they'd gobbled down the night before, and ask for coffee?

The whole idea of someone else at her beck and call made her so uncomfortable. Of course, yes, it would be great to wake up as a princess and have someone there to make her bed every day and build her bedroom fire and cook her meals and whatever else a household staff did for you, but since she wasn't a princess, she had no idea how to do this. She wasn't walking into a restaurant; she was walking downstairs in a house and asking people who were used to working for royalty to work for her, a black woman from Oakland who had celebrated her fiftieth birthday almost five years ago. Were they irritated about having to wait hand and foot on her and Maddie?

She pulled herself up straight. Hell with it. If they were, oh well. She was here, wasn't she? It's not like she was going to ask for a four-course meal, but coffee was a reasonable request. This was a trip of new experiences, wasn't it? It was time to put her bra on and do this.

She heard a crackle on the other side of the room and looked up from the note. She shook her head and laughed. There was a brand-new fire in the fireplace. Someone must have come in and made it up while she was in the shower. If the staff was irritated about waiting on her, they hadn't shown it.

Twenty minutes later, she made her way down two flights of stairs. When she got to the ground floor, she hesitated for a second and then turned left, toward the back of the house. She wasn't positive that was where the kitchen was, but it made the most sense. She'd sort of expected to see someone on her journey across the ground floor—any of the men in suits, for example—but though she heard faint music and some voices in the distance, she saw no one.

Finally, after she walked through a formal living room with furniture that looked so elaborate she was afraid to touch it, and a huge dining room with a wooden table that gleamed, she followed a narrow hallway that she was sure must lead to the kitchen. The sound of voices and of running water from that direction made her even more certain. She took a deep breath and stepped into the room with a smile on her face.

"Good morning, I'm Vivian Forest," she said to the young woman with red hair standing at the stove. Well, she was probably somewhere in her thirties, but Vivian would always call anyone in the vicinity of her daughter's age "young," no matter how old they both got. "If it's not too much trouble, can I have . . . ?"

Her voice trailed off as she looked around the room. It wasn't the huge wood beam ceiling that stopped her, or the enormous bright red stove, or the dried herbs and garlic and onion braids hanging over the big wooden table. No, it was the man standing by the back door.

His hair was short, with a touch of gray at the temples. He was wearing a shirt and tie and suit pants, but with a very cozy-looking cardigan on top instead of a jacket. He had a plaid scarf wrapped around his neck and was somehow pulling it off better than any nonmodel she'd ever seen. His skin was warm brown. And he was smiling at her like they'd been friends for years. She couldn't help but return a smile just as big.

"Ms. Forest, good morning!" Vivian's attention snapped back to the woman standing at the stove. "I just made a new pot of coffee. Would you like a cup? Or tea? I'm happy to make you whatever breakfast you want. We weren't sure what you and the other Ms. Forest would like, so I have a lot of options, but I made some fresh scones this morning if that interests you? The other Ms. Forest mentioned you enjoy them at breakfast."

Vivian couldn't decide what appealed to her more, hot coffee and fresh scones, or that man in the corner who looked like a tall mug of hot chocolate.

Why choose?

"I'd love both the coffee and a scone. Thank you so much."

Would Hot Chocolate leave? Or come farther into the room? Or just stay silent until she went away? Vivian tried to keep her mind on the woman pouring her coffee.

"I'm Julia Pepper. I'm the cook here at Sycamore Cottage. It's nice to meet you." She set the cup in a saucer and then on a tray. "I can bring the coffee and some scones into the sitting room where you ate last night, if that's convenient for you?"

Vivian would rather stay in this warm, comfortable-looking kitchen and chat with Julia and Mr. Chocolate over there, but she didn't want to disturb the running of the household.

"Oh yes, of course, that's—"

"Now Julia can introduce us," Hot Chocolate said. Good Lord, was that nickname a good one; his voice was so warm and dark and liquid. He was smiling at her again, and she smiled back.

"Ms. Forest, this is Malcolm Hudson." Julia's voice sounded amused. "He's Her Majesty's private secretary now, but he's always had a soft spot for my scones." Her Majesty. As in, the Queen. This man worked directly for the Queen? What in God's name? "Mr. Hudson, Ms. Forest."

He stepped all the way inside the kitchen to shake her hand. His big, warm hand enveloped hers and shook firmly, but not for too long. She sent up a tiny thank-you that she'd put a bra and lipstick on before coming downstairs.

"Nice to meet you, Mr. Hudson." People seemed very fond of using last names here, so she was going to go with it. When in Rome, after all. "I hope there are enough scones for both of us."

He laughed and turned to Julia.

"What do you think? Are there enough scones for both of us?"

Julia picked up a plate full of scones and presented it to him.

"I know you want all of these, but some of them are for tea, you know."

Vivian picked up her cup of coffee from the tray Julia had

been preparing. She took a sip and smiled. Julia made good coffee.

"Have you both worked for the royal family long?"

Malcolm nodded.

"We've both gone back and forth a bit, haven't we, Julia?"

Julia put a scone on a smaller plate, and set it in front of Vivian, along with tiny pots of jam and what Vivian thought might be clotted cream. She then did the same for Malcolm. Vivian watched him spread jam and the cream onto his scone. Was that how they ate them here?

"I definitely have. I've worked for a few members of the family, but I started off over at Windsor Castle." Yes, okay, of course, this nice young woman used to work at a castle. "I'm a pastry chef by training and came in at first just for a few special events, then got hired on permanently. There was some staff turnover a few years ago, and I left to go work in a restaurant, but then the Duchess lured me back, and now I work for them full-time."

Vivian spread jam and cream onto her scone like Malcolm had, and then took a bite.

"Oh my goodness, this is delicious," she said. "No wonder the Duchess lured you back."

Malcolm laughed and picked up his scone.

"Do you see why I show up at the back door with a pleading look on my face as often as possible?"

Vivian downed the rest of her coffee.

"I absolutely do. Were you also the one who made those fantastic sandwiches we had last night after we got in? I was in a dreamlike state after the flight and the long drive, but I swear they were from heaven."

Julia laughed and blushed. Oh wow, she was one of those redheads who blushed bright red like they did in books.

"They were just sandwiches, but I'm so pleased you liked them. You'll have to let me know if you have any food allergies or if there's anything I should avoid while you're here."

Vivian shook her head.

"No allergies here, and I'm sure anything you make will be wonderful."

She'd rather die before she told this nice woman what not to cook in her own kitchen. That might mean she'd get some unrecognizable food while she was here, but she could live with that. She smiled to herself; this whole having a chef cook your meals thing was more complicated than she thought it would be.

"So, Ms. Forest," he said. She seriously couldn't remember the last time someone had called her "Ms. Forest" this much. Maybe the last time she'd done career day at a high school? "Enjoying your time in the U.K. so far?"

She laughed.

"Absolutely, but my time in the U.K. so far has just been Heathrow Airport, the inside of a car, and this house. We just got in last night and came straight here."

Julia refilled Vivian's coffee cup.

"Oh no, that will never do. Ms. Forest needs a tour of the Sandringham Estate. Don't you think so, Malcolm?" Julia looked up at Malcolm with a twinkle in her eye.

Vivian shook her head.

"Please, don't feel like you have to—"

He grinned at her, then at Julia.

"Julia has a point. We can't have you thinking all of the country is like Heathrow Airport. I'd love to give you a tour of the estate. Unless you had other plans for this morning?"

She shook her head again.

"I didn't, and I'd love a tour, but are you sure you have time? Your . . . boss doesn't need you?"

He reached for a napkin and wrapped up two more scones.

"We meet in the mornings; she rarely goes off schedule."

Julia smiled at Vivian.

"Ms. Forest, lunch is at one o'clock, but feel free to drop in if you need another snack in the meantime, though one of those scones in my good napkin had better be for you."

Malcolm lifted his hands, one of which was holding on to the napkin-wrapped scones.

"Both of them can be for her if she wants! Ms. Forest is from California; she isn't used to the damp air here. She'll need something to warm her up."

Julia laughed and turned away from him. She pressed some button in the corner of the room.

"Gregory, can you please bring Ms. Forest's coat to the kitchen? Thank you."

Thirty seconds later, her driver from the night before delivered her coat and scarf to the kitchen.

"Are you ready, Ms. Forest?" Hot Chocolate / Malcolm Hudson asked.

She'd just come downstairs for coffee, and now she was going on a tour around Sandringham with the Queen's Private Secretary? Who happened to be a really attractive black man? England was treating her well so far.

"Lead the way," she said.

Chapter Two

M alcolm had no idea what had prompted him to offer
Vivian Forest a tour of Sandringham. This would ruin
his well-planned morning. He didn't give people tours, and he
didn't even know much about the Sandringham Estate. But
something about Vivian's smile had made him want to talk to
her for longer than it took to eat his scones.

Plus, he'd been feeling strangely restless this week. Maybe
it was because he was here at Sandringham, instead of at
home in London, and had been forced out of his normal rou-
tine, but he'd been fighting off boredom. Which was ridiculous, just on the face of it—he was only up here because
Parliament was being anything but boring right now—but for
some reason, he'd needed something to break the pattern he

felt stuck in. That feeling was what had made him walk over to Sycamore Cottage this morning, so he supposed playing tour guide was his punishment for his restlessness.

He glanced over at Vivian and laughed to himself. Vivian Forest, with her bright smile, glowing skin, and curvy body, looked like a reward, not a punishment. He didn't know what he'd been rewarded for, but he was grateful, nonetheless. He made a mental note to say yes to the next thing the Duchess's office asked him for.

Vivian wrapped her scarf tighter around her neck when they stepped outside.

"Cold, Ms. Forest?" he asked.

She laughed.

"Very, but I'm enjoying it. I rarely go anywhere colder than Northern California at this time of year, so it's fun to experience actual winter. I'm glad my daughter made me buy this coat, though."

He smiled at her pink cheeks and wide eyes as she looked around at the trees surrounding them, some still holding on to their leaves.

"Oh, but that brings up one more thing." She stopped and turned to him. "I don't want to be the rude American, and I'm trying to follow all of these English customs, but . . . please, call me Vivian. I haven't been called Ms. Forest this much since Maddie was in school."

Malcolm laughed. This attitude of hers was why he'd smiled as soon as Vivian had walked into the kitchen, and why he'd invited her on this tour of the estate. He'd been both surprised and delighted by her demeanor when she'd walked in. Almost all guests of the royal family fell into one of two categories: either they were full of themselves and their own consequence, and felt the need to demand things from the staff at all hours of the day just to get what they felt they deserved, or they were overcome with all of the grandeur and refused to ask the staff for anything, even though that made it impossible for the staff to do their jobs.

Vivian, however, was different. She had such a strong and joyful sense of self when she walked into the kitchen. She was neither demanding nor bashful; just friendly and inquisitive and smiling.

"It will be my pleasure, Vivian. And I'm Malcolm, by the way." She smiled.

"Hi, Malcolm, nice to meet you, and thank you for humoring me. And thank you for picking up on Julia's hint and offering to take me on this tour. I appreciate it."

Right, the tour. Hmmm.

He made a quick decision.

"Unless you object, I thought we could walk around the estate a bit and then over to Sandringham House? It's a sort of sprawling building, and we won't be able to see most of it, but even some could be interesting."

She stuck her hands in her pockets. He hoped her daughter had also gotten her mittens for this trip, along with that coat.

"That sounds lovely, thank you. Wherever we go is great; it'll be nice to stretch my legs after that long flight yesterday.

And to know a little bit about where I am—we went straight from the airport to the car to come here, and it was already dark by the time we arrived." She turned around and looked back at Sycamore Cottage. "I didn't even really know what this house looked like from the outside until now."

He turned around with her, gazed at the brick, ivy-covered cottage, and smiled.

"I've always appreciated this cottage," he said. "I was so pleased when the Duke and Duchess moved in."

She shook her head and laughed.

"That's another cultural discrepancy I've learned since my less than twenty-four hours in England—you call things 'cottages' that are about six times the size of my house."

Okay, she had a point there. He grinned at her.

"Just wait until you see the thing we call a house. Then you'll understand why that's a cottage in comparison."

They walked together down the tree-lined paths for a while. He wished for the first time in his life he knew more about trees; that way he'd be able to tell Vivian about what was around them. Granted, at this time of year, most of the trees were bare. Instead of making a fool out of himself by rambling about trees, he asked her how her flight was.

Her smile widened as she answered him.

"Much better than I thought it would be," she said. "It was definitely the longest flight I've ever taken, but also the most comfortable."

They chatted for a while about air travel and how her drive

from Heathrow up to Sandringham was, until they turned the corner. He gestured in front of them.

"That's Sandringham House." Only part of the huge, sprawling redbrick structure was visible from where they stood, but it was impressive from any vantage point. "It could probably fit at least twenty Sycamore Cottages inside of it, with room to spare."

She stopped and stared. He stood next to her. It really was an enormous structure, when you took a step back and paid attention.

"Wow. Good Lord. You work in that building?"

He walked on, and she followed.

"Not most of the time." He kept his face blank. "Most of the time I work in Buckingham Palace, which is even larger."

Vivian laughed again.

"Slumming it this week, hmm?"

He glanced around them.

"Oh yes, absolutely." They both laughed. "Her Majesty is only here a couple of months out of the year, and most of that time there's only skeleton staff up here with her. I usually wouldn't be with her at Sandringham so close to Christmas, but it's been an unusual year."

He'd been irritated that all of the nonsense in Parliament made him have to spend this much time in Norfolk in December, but meeting Vivian Forest was a bit of a silver lining.

She raised an eyebrow at him.

"Does that mean you're not always where the Queen is?" She shook her head. "If that question is too nosy, please excuse me and pretend I didn't ask it; jet lag has taken away my filter."

He smiled at her.

"It's perfectly all right. I'm usually based out of Buckingham Palace—I only travel with her to her other estates when circumstances warrant."

She nodded. He could tell she wanted to ask what the circumstances were, but instead she took her phone out of her pocket.

"Is it okay if I take pictures?" she asked. "Actually, are you sure it's okay that I'm walking around here, with the Queen around?"

He laughed and nodded.

"Don't worry, the Duke and Duchess often have guests at Sycamore Cottage. The staff—and the Queen—are all aware that you and the other Ms. Forest are here."

She smiled at him and snapped a few pictures. The wind blew her hair against her face, and he had the wild urge to brush it away. He took a step back from her and cleared his throat. "So, Ms. Forest—excuse me, Vivian. You're from California, is that right? Did you grow up there?"

She nodded.

"I've lived there my whole life. I thought about moving away for a while—I'd decided that after college I'd try to move to the South, or maybe even travel abroad. But life got in the way."

Most of the time when people said things like this, they looked sad, or at least wistful. Vivian just seemed matter-of-fact.

"But I love California, and I have no idea what it would be like to live anywhere else. Though I love the glimpses of other states and countries that I've seen; I hope I get to travel more when I retire."

"What kind of work do you do?" he asked. He'd learned Americans always wanted you to ask them this question—he usually avoided doing so, but he wanted to put Vivian at ease.

She paused for a moment.

"I'm a social worker. At a hospital in Oakland," she said.

That was probably why it was so easy to talk to her.

She stuck her hands deeper in her pockets. It really was cold today.

"I have my gloves with me." He touched her elbow. "If you're cold and need to wear something on your hands, I mean."

She laughed and shook her head.

"Oh no, thank you. It's just that I'm so used to a sunny day and a bright blue sky translating to warmth, so I keep expecting it to warm up, then I remember it doesn't work like that in most places."

He was glad she had that warm coat and scarf, at least. It was almost as cold inside Sandringham House as it was outside.

"Will you be all right to walk around outside for a while?" he asked. "Or do you want to head straight for the house?"

She shook her head.

"It's nice to be outside. Yesterday I was in airports and airplanes and cars all day; it's good to have some fresh air, even if it's cold."

They took a roundabout route up to Sandringham House. She seemed to enjoy looking around at the vast, well-maintained, tree-lined estate, even though he didn't have much detail to tell her about it.

"Had you been to the U.K. before?" he asked her.

She shook her head.

"Never. But I'm thrilled to be here."

He smiled at her.

"Well, I hope you enjoy your holiday. Please let me know if there's anything I can do for you while you're here."

Why did he say that? Being a concierge for some American tourists—even if they were the guests of the Duke and Duchess—wasn't his job.

She smiled at him and shook her head.

Ah. He did it so she'd smile at him again. He must have lost his mind. A fifty-two-year-old man and he was acting like a teenager with a crush.

"That's so nice of you to offer, but you don't have to do that. Plus, I'm only here for about a week—we're here at Sandringham through Christmas, then Maddie and I are spending a few days in London before we fly home."

"What are you planning to do in London?" he asked.

She laughed.

"I've honestly left all of the planning to Maddie, and I barely know anything about London, so it'll all be fresh and exciting for me. She did say we're staying at a very fancy hotel, which should be fun."

That smile was still on her face. It made him want London to be perfect for her.

"Well, please do ask if you have questions about anything; I'd be happy to help. And now, welcome to Sandringham House." They walked under the big archway in the drive and through the wide front doors. He nodded at the footmen who opened the doors for them. "I usually go in and out one of the side doors, but I decided you needed the full experience for your first time here."

She stopped in the entryway with a look of awe on her face.

"Wow." She turned around in a circle, and he turned with her. Right in front of them was the massive Christmas tree, blanketed in white lights, which almost touched the two-story-high ceiling. On either side of the carpeted spiral staircase were two sitting rooms, filled with antique carpets, golden lamps, and brocade couches. The floor was ivory-colored tile. Everything gleamed like it was made of gold.

It was good to see this house through new eyes. It really was a lot to take in. He led her toward the drawing room. She followed him slowly, still looking around.

"Architecturally, this building is a bit of a hodgepodge, but it's still quite impressive."

She trailed her hand along the banister as they walked by the stairs.

"Impressive and overwhelming." She looked up and down the hallway, both sides of which had guns mounted along the walls. "And you work in buildings like this every day?"

He nodded.

"I do. At first I was awed by it every day, and now I'm used to it, for the most part. It strikes me every time something major happens—when there's a state dinner, or a royal wedding, something like that—but things can become normal to you so quickly. And I've been working in and around these buildings for, all told, well over fifteen years now." He smiled at her. "But sometimes I look around and I can't believe I work amidst all of this."

He took her into the drawing room, to see the painted ceilings and the art on the walls, then into the dining room, to see the tapestries hanging from the walls. She walked close to the tapestries.

"These tapestries are like something I've seen in a museum," she said. He noticed that she kept her hands clasped behind her back. "The work that must have gone into these . . . all the detail. How extraordinary."

He'd never inspected the tapestries that closely before, but now he stood next to her to look at them. She was right—so many of those tiny stitches created this artwork. What a feat.

Vivian made a circle of the room before she returned to his side.

"It's like being inside a museum, except with no one else there."

He looked around the room and laughed.

"That's exactly what it's like."

They wandered through most of the main rooms, both up and downstairs. He took her to see the main dining room, but it was a bevy of activity with the staff getting ready for Christmas, so they just stood at the door and watched for a while. They went through the ballroom, where she gasped at the incredibly high ceilings and crystal chandeliers. They turned back down the central corridor toward the main staircase, and he saw Vivian stare at the walls lined with many different types of weapons.

"So medieval," she said under her breath. He turned back and grinned at her, and she grinned back.

He'd been so consumed with work this year that he hadn't stopped to enjoy himself in a while. This past hour with Vivian Forest had been the most fun he'd had in months. He liked walking with her. He liked talking to her. He hadn't felt like this since . . .

He rolled his eyes at himself. One pretty black woman his age turns up, and he starts acting like his teenage nephew.

"Can I ask you a very basic question?" she said, when they reached the top of the stairs.

He stopped and smiled at her.

"Certainly."

She looked down, then back at him.

"You'll have to forgive me. I don't know much about the monarchy—what does the Private Secretary to the Queen actually do?"

He laughed.

"Don't worry, lots of people don't know the answer to that question. Many things: the biggest role is to advise the monarch on political and government issues. She gets a box of government documents to read through every day, and does so without fail. And with, well, current events being what they are, we always have plenty to discuss."

Vivian nodded.

"Like with a lot of things about England, at first your system seems similar to ours, then when you dig deeper, it's like it's all in a completely different language."

He lowered his voice.

"Don't tell anyone this, but I worked for a member of Parliament early in my career, and for the Foreign Office for years after that, and I still sometimes get confused about politics here."

She laughed again, and he smiled at her.

"But the job is also a lot of work dealing with her diary"—he saw the perplexed look on Vivian's face—"or her calendar, as Americans call it—all of her public and private engagements."

"So lots of juggling, in other words." She smiled at him. "That makes it even more kind that you took the time out of your schedule to give me a tour. Thank you."

He almost laughed. It had nothing to do with kindness; it was all selfishness on his part. He'd enjoyed this more than he'd enjoyed anything in a while.

"It's my pleasure, Ms. Forest." He winked at her, and she smiled.

He stopped in front of one of the big picture windows at the back of the house.

"You can see the stables from here."

She gazed out the window toward where he was pointing.

"Oh wow, and there's someone riding a horse!" She laughed. "Sorry, I'm sure this is normal for you, but it's wild for me to see people on horseback like it's nothing. The closest I've ever been to a horse in real life, other than a zoo, was probably one of those carriage horses they have in New York City."

He bowed his head to her.

"Oh, we can't have that. I'd love to take you to meet some horses while you're here, if you have time. Maybe tomorrow?"

What in God's name was he saying? He had enough on his plate for the next week; he didn't need to keep playing tour guide. He had a whole list of detailed plans for tomorrow: go over all of the scheduled engagements for the royal family for the next three months, check on the progression of the Trooping the Colour logistics, deal with that memo he'd meant to read for ages, et cetera.

Granted . . . none of that was time sensitive. He *was* in a bit of a holding pattern right now, just waiting for news. He had plenty of time to do all of those tasks.

Vivian smiled at him.

"I'd love that," she said.

As they walked on, she turned to him with a question on her face, then turned away.

"Was there something else?" he asked.

She shook her head.

"No, it's too personal of a question. We just met each other an hour ago."

He opened up the napkin he'd been carrying since they left Sycamore Cottage and handed her one of Julia's scones.

"We met over these scones; you get one free question. Didn't you know the old English superstition?"

She shook her head and laughed at him but took the scone.

"I know you all think Americans are gullible about the British, and we will probably believe anything you say about many things, especially when you say it in that incredible accent, but that's where I draw the line. But fine, I'll ask anyway: Are there other black people who work for the Queen?"

A lot of people had tried to ask him this question, but they'd asked it so euphemistically he'd been able to pretend he didn't understand what they were asking, even when they'd rephrased it three or four times. He smiled at those memories. That had frustrated those people so much.

Strangely, though, he didn't mind Vivian Forest asking him this. Maybe it was because of the way she'd asked it—so up front and without any dancing around. Or maybe it was just because he liked her.

"A few, but not many. When I worked for her the first time, I was the only one on the personal staff—since I've come back, there have been a few more, but . . . only a few."

He led her in the direction of his office on the far side of the house.

"Why did you leave? And why did you come back?" She shook her head. "I'm sorry, I keep asking so many questions. You don't have to answer that."

He laughed.

"I don't mind. I left the first time because I received a job offer in the private sector that I couldn't refuse." One which had paid him almost three times the salary he'd received as an assistant private secretary. Working for the Queen meant many things, but good pay wasn't one of them. "I worked for a consulting firm for years; I was skeptical about how much I'd like the job at first, but it turned out I enjoy it a great deal. But I came back because my former boss had some health issues that caused him to resign suddenly, and Her Majesty needed someone experienced to jump into the private secretary role, so she called me. At first I said no, but she invited me for tea to discuss it further, and"—he smiled at Vivian—"she's very good at pleading her case. So here I am. I warned her that I couldn't promise to stay here forever—I would like to go back to the private sector at some point—but it's been good to be back."

Vivian nodded. He could tell she'd really been listening to him. She hesitated for a moment, but finally asked her question.

"Are you the first? Black private secretary, I mean?"

He nodded slowly and tried not to let his face reflect the rush of pride he felt.

"And that's another reason I said yes."

He spent his days immersed in this job and didn't think about that too often. What an accomplishment it was, and everything it had taken for him to achieve it. Not just the years of hard work, but all of the tiny insults and jokes he'd had to ignore, all of the naysayers, the hundreds of times he'd kept a straight face and a low voice when he wanted to pound on the table and yell.

He opened the door to his small office.

"And here's where I work—less glamorous than the rest of the house, but it's enough for what I need."

She looked around and smiled at the painting on his wall and the photographs of his family on his desk. She picked up one of them.

"Your son?" she asked him.

He shook his head.

"My nephew. My sister's son. His father died when he was young, and I suppose I've been a bit of a surrogate dad for him. He's a great kid—well, he's not a kid anymore, but I'll never stop thinking of him that way."

Vivian laughed.

"I do the same thing with Maddie, and she's in her thirties. How old is he now?"

He smiled.

"Nineteen. He'll be off to Oxford next year."

Vivian raised her eyebrows at him.

"Following in your footsteps?"

How had she figured that out?

"Yes, but how did you know?"

She grinned at him.

"It was something about that look of pride in your eyes when you said it."

He laughed.

"I try not to be so obvious, but since I'm bragging about him"—he gestured at the painting over his desk—"Miles painted that for me a few years ago. It's the river in Scotland where we often go fishing together. I know there are lots of priceless paintings in this building, but this one is my favorite." Miles's painting was usually on the wall of his office at Buckingham Palace, but he'd brought it down here for the week. These walls were too bare and dreary without it.

Vivian contemplated the painting, then smiled at him.

"I can see why it's your favorite."

Malcolm was looking forward to seeing Miles at Christmas. He'd seen very little of his nephew over the past few months. Most of that was his own fault—work had been busier than usual this fall—but whenever he'd texted Miles, the boy had been either in the middle of painting, and so didn't text back for hours, or more likely, with his new girlfriend, the one Malcolm's sister, Sarah, hated. In their texts recently, Miles had hinted that he had some big surprise to tell him about at Christmas—probably that he was going to move in with the new girlfriend. He shook his head and sighed. He'd be the one to have to smooth that over with Sarah, like he usually had to do with Miles's escapades.

She walked over to the window and looked out.

"You have a lovely view here, Malcolm. This estate really is beautiful."

He stood next to her. The window wasn't that big, so he was so close to her they were almost touching.

"It is."

His phone rang, and she stepped aside. He glanced down at who was calling and shook his head.

"I don't have to get that." He looked at the clock next to his phone and had a jolt. It had been over two hours since he'd left the Sycamore Cottage kitchen with Vivian. How had they managed to talk for that long?

Vivian looked at her watch and took a step back.

"Oh! I didn't realize how late it had gotten. I'm sorry for taking you away from your work for so long. I should walk back to Sycamore Cottage. Maddie is probably looking for me." She looked back up at him. "Thank you so much, Malcolm, for the walk and the tour and the conversation. It was a great first morning in England."

They left his office together.

"I can walk you back to Sycamore Cottage," he said.

She tilted her head.

"Do you really have time for that?"

He hesitated, and her smile got wider. Finally he gave up and smiled back at her.

"As a matter of fact . . . no, but . . ."

They both laughed.

"I can walk back on my own, I promise," she said. "Just point me in the right direction, and maybe warn the security guards that a middle-aged black American woman is wandering around the grounds of a royal estate."

He laughed as they went down the back stairs.

"No need, I told you they know you're here. But I'm going to take you out the side door—we took the long way up to the house today, because I wanted you to see the whole thing, but it's faster to get back to Sycamore Cottage from this door."

She smiled.

"It helps that I know what it looks like now." She pulled out her phone. "And those pictures I took on our walk here will come in handy to get me home."

He paused by the door.

"Did you trail scone crumbs, too, so you could find your way home?"

She winked at him.

"See, I knew I was inside of a fairy tale."

He opened the side door for her, and the cold air rushed in at them.

"Have a safe walk back, Ms. Forest. I'm counting on that trip to the stables tomorrow."

She grinned.

"Thank you, Mr. Hudson. I look forward to it."

She walked away and waved at him. He turned to go inside, still with a smile on his face.

Chapter Three

Vivian's walk back to Sycamore Cottage took only about fifteen minutes. How was that possible, when her walk from Sycamore Cottage to Sandringham House with Malcolm had taken so much longer?

Well, they'd walked the long way around, after all. And that house was enormous. Plus, he'd had to stop and show her things on the way in, like the . . . Okay, she couldn't remember anymore what he'd stopped to show her; she just remembered how entertained she'd been.

She hadn't lost track of time like that talking to a man in years. It had probably been since the beginning of her relationship with Ray, which had fizzled out on both sides a few years ago. She knew this couldn't be the beginning of any sort of relationship—not even a fling, since she was sleeping in a Duchess's guest room across the hall from her *daughter*—but she'd missed having someone to talk to. Someone to flirt with. Someone to laugh with. Someone—a male someone—who clearly enjoyed her company.

She had no idea if Malcolm really was going to get in touch with her to show her the stables, but she bet that he would. She'd seen that interested look in a man's eye enough times to recognize it. If she had even a few more hours of that during her time in England, what an unexpected bonus that would be.

She walked up the front steps to Sycamore Cottage, still smiling, and said hello to the suit who opened the door before she'd even been able to knock.

"Ms. Forest." He nodded at her.

She smiled at him.

"Good afternoon . . . I'm sorry, what's your name?"

She wasn't sure if she was supposed to ask questions like this, but she wasn't in the habit of letting people open her doors and cook for her without knowing their names. Of course, she wasn't in the habit of letting people open her doors at all, but she knew the names of all of the cafeteria workers at the hospital, and all of the janitors, too. This guy might wear a suit, but that didn't make him invisible.

"James, ma'am."

She nodded at him.

"Good afternoon, James."

Maddie came into the hallway.

"I thought I heard your voice. Where did you go this morning? You look all smiling and windblown; did you have a nice walk? Are you ready for lunch?"

Vivian unwound the scarf from around her neck, and James took it and her coat from her.

"More than ready. I'm starving."

Maddie led her back toward the kitchen.

"Great. Lunch is just us. The Duke and Duchess are off doing a family thing this afternoon. I can't relax for long; I have a bunch of tiny alterations to do that I want to make sure to get right, so I'll be booked most of the afternoon, if that's okay."

Vivian nodded.

"Of course that's okay; you're here to work. I'll keep myself occupied, don't worry."

She pulled her phone out of her pocket to check if Jo had texted back.

> Doing great here, don't worry about me. You'd better be having a great time in England!!!

"How's everyone at home?" Maddie asked.

"Okay, I hope. Aunt Jo says she is, anyway. But she might just be saying that."

Maddie put her arm around Vivian's shoulder.

"Aunt Jo is fine, Mom. I'm sure she wants you to relax and not worry about her."

Vivian laughed.

"That's just what she told me to do. Are you two conspiring against me?"

"Conspiring *for* you, maybe," Maddie said.

They walked into a little breakfast room Vivian hadn't noticed before, where Julia was setting lunch out on the table.

"Ms. Forest, hello again. Did you have a nice walk with Mr. Hudson?"

Vivian saw Maddie's eyes on her.

"I did, thank you. He gave me a lovely tour of the grounds and the house, though I'm sure we only saw a small fraction of what there is. And we enjoyed those scones of yours a great deal."

Julia laughed.

"He's always like that about those scones. I tease him like he's not allowed to have them, but I always make extras so he can have some, and I wager he knows that." She gestured to the small, round table. "Please, sit down. Your lunch is all ready."

Julia bustled back to the kitchen, and Vivian and Maddie sat at the table.

Before Maddie could ask the question Vivian knew was coming, Julia brought bowls of steaming potato soup and a platter of roast beef sandwiches to the table.

"I thought you'd need something cozy and warming, and you said how much you enjoyed those sandwiches last night." She poured them water from a pitcher on the table. "If you need anything else, just ring the bell here."

Vivian and Maddie both thanked her, and she disappeared.

Vivian tasted the soup. She was doubtful about it—in her experience, potato soup tended to be heavy and bland. But wow, this was creamy and flavorful and just what she needed after a walk outside in northern England in December.

"Oh wow, this soup is great."

Maddie put her spoon into the soup but didn't taste it.

"Hey, Mom?"

Vivian looked up at her, a mock-innocent expression on her face.

"Yes, Maddie?"

"Who is 'Mr. Hudson'?"

Vivian laughed, more at how predictable her daughter was than the question itself. When Maddie was little, Vivian had kept her life with her daughter very separate from any romantic relationships. That had infuriated Maddie, who since the age of seven had wanted to know if her mother was dating anyone and if not, why not. Vivian had always refused to tell her—which had just infuriated Maddie more. Even though her daughter was a grown woman now, she'd never really gotten out of the habit of keeping her personal life a secret.

But she supposed she had to answer this question. She and Malcolm weren't dating; she would probably never see him again.

Though she really hoped she did.

"Malcolm Hudson works over at Sandringham House. He was in the kitchen this morning chatting with Julia when I came down for breakfast, and he offered to give me a little tour of the grounds while you were occupied. Satisfied?"

"What does he do over at Sandringham House?" Maddie was obviously not satisfied. "What was he doing in the kitchen here?"

There was no real way to avoid answering these questions, was there?

"He was in the kitchen because he and Julia have known each other for years, and he came over to say hi to her. And he's the private secretary to the Queen."

Maddie dropped her spoon.

"The what to the Queen?"

Vivian carefully didn't roll her eyes.

"The private secretary." She took another sip of the soup.

Maddie stared at her.

"That's a big deal kind of job, Mom!"

Vivian took a bite of her sandwich.

"Yes, I gathered that," she said. Sometimes she really enjoyed irritating her daughter like this.

"Okay, but then, why did he give you a tour? Doesn't he have more important things to do with his time?"

Vivian was pretty sure he had many more important things to do with his time, which made her even more pleased he'd taken two hours out of his schedule to wander around and chat and eat scones with her today. But saying that to Maddie would cause her to ask a million more unanswerable questions, so instead, she just shrugged.

"It's Christmastime. I think he had some unexpected free time, so he decided to fill it by entertaining the nearby

American. It was a really nice walk, even though it was freezing outside. I'm glad you made me get this coat; it and my boots were the only things that kept me from turning into a Popsicle." Vivian had to deflect Maddie before she asked even more about this man. Luckily, she knew just how to do it. "How was your morning with the Duchess? Did the clothes get delivered okay? Did you guys make some good decisions?"

Maddie nodded eagerly.

"Yeah, it was a great morning. All of the clothes got delivered, thank God, and the staff here did a fantastic job listening to my very specific directions about how to hang them up. I always feel like an asshole when I have to give instructions like that to other people, because I get so particular and detailed about everything. But maybe in royal households they're used to people being exacting, because they don't seem to hate me, even after my three-page email about ten different things to do with ten different navy blue dresses."

Vivian laughed and poured more water for both of them.

"Well, that's good. I've seen how you get when people don't listen to your very specific instructions. People like me, for example."

Maddie rolled her eyes and went on.

"Amelia usually spends a week in England every two or so months to work with the Duchess and plan for all of the upcoming events, but she hasn't been here in three months, so I have a lot of work cut out for me in the next few days, but I think it'll be a lot of fun. A lot of pressure, too, but I'm up to the challenge, especially with you here." She grinned at Vivian. "Tomorrow we might head into the town to do some shopping for an hour or so. Let me know if you want to come."

Vivian smiled to herself.

"I'll think about it, but I might want to just relax here"—she looked at her daughter pointedly—"like you keep telling me I have to. And it will be nice to hang out and read; I don't get much time to do that at home."

That was all true, but she hoped she'd have other plans tomorrow. Plans Maddie didn't need to know about.

Malcolm spent the rest of the day attempting to do nationally important work, but all he could think about was Vivian. He knew he was being ridiculous, but for once, he didn't care. He'd spent two hours with an attractive, interesting, charming woman, and it had been the happiest and most relaxed two hours he'd spent in months.

Maybe years.

Had she taken him seriously when he'd suggested going to the stables? Because he'd meant every word of it, but maybe she'd just been polite?

Well, there was one way to find out.

He packed up a notepad when he left the office for the day, and once he was settled into his hotel room in town, he sat down at the desk to write Vivian a note.

It felt unnecessarily formal to do it this way, but he had no other way of getting in touch with her, and he knew a note left for her at Sycamore Cottage would reach her. He decided to lean into the formality of it all, since he'd gotten the impression today that it amused her.

The next morning, he copied out his final draft of the note onto his official stationery and slipped it into an envelope.

Ms. Forest,

I'd like to request the pleasure of your company at 14:00—2:00 p.m. to you—this afternoon at the Sandringham House stables. If you are agreed, I'll call for you at Sycamore Cottage. The horses look forward to making your acquaintance.

Sincerely,
Malcolm Hudson

He scrawled her name on the outside of the envelope and pressed a button on his desk to summon a footman to his office. It felt very Victorian to do it like this, but when one worked in a palace, one may as well make use of artifacts from the past on occasion.

"Please bring this over to Sycamore Cottage, if you would," he said once the footman finally arrived at his door. "If there is a reply, please bring it back to me directly."

The footman nodded.

"Very good, Mr. Hudson."

He smiled as he walked down to his daily meeting with the Queen.

A few minutes after he got back to his office, there was a knock at his door. He looked up to see the footman. He kept his face blank.

"Yes?"

"I have a reply for you, Mr. Hudson," he said. He stepped forward and handed it to Malcolm, who dropped it on his desk like it didn't matter at all.

"Very good. Thank you."

The footman nodded and left. As soon as he'd turned away, Malcolm pulled the letter out of the envelope.

Mr. Hudson,

Thank you for your kind invitation to introduce me to the Sandringham horses. Nothing could delight me more than to visit the stables with you. I look forward to your call this afternoon.

Kind regards,
Ms. Vivian Forest

He dropped the letter on his desk and laughed out loud. He had a feeling this afternoon would be fun.

He picked up the phone and called down to the stable manager.

When Malcolm walked over to Sycamore Cottage a few

hours later, he was halfway up the path to the kitchen door before he realized he had to go to the front door for this visit. He couldn't send over a letter on his heavy stationery and then make Vivian come meet him in the kitchen, no matter how great that kitchen was. So he doubled back around and walked up the steps to the front door. Before he could knock, the door swung open.

"Mr. Hudson." The butler reached for his coat. "You're expected."

He handed over his coat.

"Thank you, James."

James showed him into the sitting room, where Vivian sat in front of a fire, drinking a cup of tea, and with a plate piled full of scones in front of her, and small bowls full of cream and jam.

"Julia found out you were coming by to pick me up, and before I could blink, a mountain of scones appeared. Do you have time for tea and a scone before we leave?"

He sat down next to her.

"I always have time for Julia's scones."

She poured him a cup of tea.

"No milk or sugar in my tea, thank you." He looked over the tea tray. "I'm surprised Julia didn't make you any more of those sandwiches you love."

A smile danced around her lips.

"She did, but between me and the Duke, we ate them all."

He laughed out loud.

"Knowing the Duke as I do, that does not surprise me." He

looked around. "Are he and the Duchess home? Is your daughter here?"

He had been wondering if her daughter would be here when he came to take her over to the stables. He was curious about Maddie; he knew about her job and her background, obviously—it was part of his job to know that—but not what she was like as a person. All he knew was that she'd insisted on bringing her mother with her to England for Christmas, and at this juncture, he was very grateful to her for that.

She shook her head.

"No, she and the Duchess went into town to go shopping right after lunch. I think the Duke is off with others in the family."

She'd finished her scone, so he took the last bite of his.

"Well, if they're all having outings today, I'm pleased you are, too." He stood up and offered her his hand. "Shall we?"

She took his hand and stood up.

"We shall."

Had she wanted to go shopping instead of going to the stables?

When they got outside, he turned to her.

"I'm sorry if I kept you from a shopping trip in town with your daughter and the Duchess," he said.

Vivian shook her head.

"No need—they had a very specific mission, and I would have been in the way. Plus, I wouldn't turn down the chance to visit the Sandringham stables this afternoon for the world."

He turned to her, his eyebrows raised.

"For the world?" he quoted back to her. That had a good sound to it.

She looked down, but then looked up straight into his eyes, the smile still hovering around her lips.

"When am I ever going to have the chance to do this again?" she asked. "I've never been to any stables before in my life, and to get invited to see the stables at Sandringham? I'm thrilled." She glanced at him and grimaced. "And also slightly terrified."

He'd assumed that last part, from the look of half wonder, half horror on her face when she'd seen the stables from a distance.

"There's nothing to be terrified about," he said. "The horses will be lovely to you, I promise, and so will the staff."

Would she be open to getting on a horse? Would the stable master give her the chance? For some reason, he was very much hoping she'd be able to have this opportunity.

She raised an eyebrow at him.

"Oh, you can speak for horses now?"

He nodded seriously.

"The Queen's horses are monarchists; they would never dare to mistreat a guest of the royal family."

They looked at each other and laughed.

Chapter Four

V ivian was strangely nervous about this trip to the stables,
despite what she'd said to Malcolm. She hadn't lied to
him—she knew there was no way she'd forgive herself if she'd
had the option to see the horses of the actual Queen of England
and had gone back to America without doing so. But horses
had always intimidated her. They were so big and powerful . . .
and expensive. Even though it should have been all of the servants and the huge amounts of land and people throwing
around royal titles like it was normal, it was when Malcolm had
casually pointed out the stables to her that had made her realize
what a different kind of life she'd stepped into.

She turned to Malcolm as they walked down the path.

"Is it odd for you, this whole monarchy thing?" When he

raised his eyebrows, she shook her head. "Sorry, I know that seems like it came out of nowhere. It's just that it's all so foreign to me. The whole idea of having people who, simply by the nature of their birth, get to rule the country, no matter what kind of person they are, is so contrary to everything I know. I understand that 'rule' overstates it these days, but you know what I mean. And I get that most British people don't even think about the monarchy, but you . . ."

"I live it," he said. "It's true; unlike most Brits, the monarchy is part of my daily life. And I'm used to it, and I don't think about it much, except for the times when I do, then it hits me how . . . strange it all is."

They both laughed, Vivian out of relief more than anything else. She'd been worried that she'd offended him, that she was the loud American, coming in and staying on a royal estate and then spouting off about the people who had brought her here. Thank goodness he wasn't mad.

"It can be comforting, especially when politics in general is a disaster—at least there's some permanence in this world. And since politics has been a disaster more than once during my time with Her Majesty, I'm more used to that than the alternative. And I like the whole ritual of it all. My nephew, Miles, always makes fun of how conservative I am"—he winked at her—"with a small c, that is. And I suppose it's true; I'm a person who tends to like stability, tradition, security." He laughed. "Miles says I'm a snob, but I prefer to think of it as being wary of taking unnecessary risks. But—especially during times when foreign royals come to visit, and there are other queens and kings around, and they walk together into rooms and there's a whole procession of people bowing to them—it all feels unbelievably absurd. Even though I'm always one of the people automatically bowing when they walk into a room."

She could just picture an entire room of people bowing to a person standing at the front of it. The whole idea felt ridiculous.

"Wow. That must be so strange to see. And to do."

He nodded at her.

"You have no idea."

He stopped and looked around.

"How in the world did you get me to say all of this, on royal land no less? I've kept a stone face about these matters for years. Thank goodness the bulk of the family doesn't arrive for two more days, otherwise I'd be terrified someone would have heard that ill-considered rant about the institution that keeps me employed." He peered into her eyes. "Do you have some sort of magic social worker powers, Ms. Forest?"

She looked straight back at him.

"Oh absolutely, I always have. Why did you think I went into social work in the first place?"

He laughed at her and walked on.

"Anyway, no more talk about You Know What for the next hour at least, please. I need to stay employed long enough to finish taking you around the stables."

He bowed and offered her his arm, and she laughed and took it.

"I have a feeling, Mr. Hudson, that you're remarkably good at your job, and it would take a great deal for you to lose it."

He grinned at her.

"You may have a point there. Especially at this time of the year, and with Parliament in chaos once again, in any event," he said. "But while I don't plan to stay in this job for the rest of my working life, I do want any decision to leave it to be mine. God save the Queen, et cetera." He flashed a smile at her, then looked away. "You don't have much experience in cold weather, do you? You should be wearing a hat."

She accepted his change of subject, even though she was dying to talk about all of this more.

"I have one in my pocket, but I'm not cold enough for it right now."

That was definitely a lie. But she knew what hats did to her hair, and she was too vain to let this attractive man see her hair all over the place.

He looked delicious in his hat, though, especially when he smiled at her like that. She was very glad he'd put it on at the door of Sycamore Cottage.

After ten more minutes of walking and talking about many things that did not involve the British monarchy, they arrived at the Sandringham stables, aka—she held back a giggle—the Royal Stud.

"Wow." They stopped outside the stables, and she took in just how big they were. From what she could tell from the outside, they were probably the size of a few city blocks at home.

"Wait until you see the inside," Malcolm said.

They walked in the open door, and she stopped again to look around. The smell hit her all at once: animals and leather and hay, and yes, manure.

A man in knee-high boots walked toward them, and Malcolm let go of her arm as he reached out to shake his hand.

"Vivian, this is Tim. He's the stable manager here and has been for years. Tim, this is Ms. Vivian Forest. This is all new to her."

Tim shook Malcolm's hand and turned to her. He had a ruddy, wrinkled face, salt-and-pepper hair, and wore a huge smile.

"Nice to meet you, Ms. Forest, and welcome to the Sandringham stables. Ever ridden a horse?"

She laughed and shook her head.

"Oh definitely not. I've probably only ever been this close to a horse on a handful of occasions."

He chuckled.

"Well, this is going to be a treat for you, now, isn't it? Let's go introduce you to Polly."

Tim strode away without another word. Vivian glanced up at Malcolm. Now she was nervous about this whole excursion again. But he gave her a reassuring smile and tucked her arm in his once more. They followed Tim toward the other end of the . . . Was it one stable they were in? Were there multiple stables? Or was every small room that a horse was in called a stable? She didn't know the answers to any of those questions. She should have asked Malcolm to clarify the terminology before they arrived.

They came out near a fenced-in area and followed Tim into another big building that housed horses; whether that was stables or a stable, she had no idea.

"Good afternoon, girl," Tim said to a warm brown horse right near the entrance. "Aren't you looking lovely today? Are you ready for some visitors?"

Vivian and Malcolm hovered behind him. The horses were so beautiful—sleek, shiny, and she loved seeing their tails twitch back and forth, and their warm, glossy manes.

They were also big.

Very big. Taller than both Malcolm and Tim big. And so strong. These weren't animals to play with or coo over; these were animals that could kill you. She would honestly be very happy to hide behind Malcolm for the rest of her time in these stables and just look at the horses without being too close to them—or, God forbid, having to touch them.

"Now, we're going to slip inside," Tim said.

"Inside? Inside there? With the horse, too?"

Tim and Malcolm both laughed. She hadn't been joking. Could they not see how big these horses were?

"Yes, we're going to go inside her stall. Don't worry, she's very gentle and she loves people. This is why I thought we should start with Polly."

Tim unhooked the door to the stall and walked inside first. Malcolm held out his arm for her to precede him. Oh God.

She was here, wasn't she? What was she going to do, chicken out of doing this? She took a deep breath and followed Tim inside the horse's stall.

"Do you have a dog, Vivian?" Tim asked her.

She shook her head. She felt Malcolm's comforting presence behind her.

"I used to. Ashby. She was a great dog. I've been thinking about getting another, but it just hasn't been the right time."

Tim nodded.

"Ashby will make this easier. Just think of Polly as a great big version of Ashby, or other dogs you've loved. She likes people to pet her, and feed her treats, and give her walks, and tell her she's a good girl, just like a great dog."

Vivian felt her shoulders relax at that description.

"Okay. Okay, that makes sense," she said.

"Good." Tim reached over and handed her something, and she took it automatically, without looking to see what it was. She opened up her hand and found a sugar cube.

"Do horses really like these?" she asked. They always had in the books Vivian used to read to Maddie when she was little, but she'd thought that could just be a thing in books.

"Close your hand, walk a little closer to her head, and slowly lift your hand up to her. You'll see how much she likes it."

Vivian turned and looked up at Malcolm. She didn't know if he could see the panic in her eyes. She also didn't know if she wanted him to see it or not.

Either way, he stuck close to her as she took a few steps to the left and then raised her hand toward Polly. For a few seconds, nothing happened, but then the horse bent her head down and nuzzled Vivian's fist. She laughed and opened her hand, and Polly licked the sugar cube right out of her palm.

"Oh wow!" Vivian said. Polly bent her head back down and nuzzled Vivian's hand again. "Sorry, sweetie, there's no more in here."

"Isn't she great?" Tim said.

Vivian smiled up at Polly, and she swore the horse smiled back down at her.

"What a sweetheart."

She turned to Tim.

"Where are the sugar cubes? Can I have another one for her, please?"

Tim pulled a cube out of one of his many pockets and slipped it in her hand.

"There are more where those came from. I was thinking, since it's such a nice day today, that we could take her out into the field and give her a little exercise?"

Vivian smiled. Only a British person would describe today's weather, which was in the high thirties at the maximum, as "such a nice day." But she supposed the sun was out.

"Sure, that sounds great," she said.

Vivian and Malcolm stepped out of the stall so Tim could lead Polly out. Malcolm put his hand on Vivian's shoulder and smiled down at her.

"How are you enjoying your first experience with horses?" he asked.

He'd been worried for a while when they first came into

the stables; as soon as they saw the horses, Vivian's whole body had tensed up. When they'd walked into Polly's stable, he'd been really afraid she would turn around and go right back out again. But nothing had been as bad as that panicked look she'd given him when Tim had handed her the sugar for the horse. Malcolm had been about five seconds from leaping to her rescue when she'd finally reached her hand up to Polly.

"I'm glad we came," she said. "At first I was . . . concerned, about, you know, being this close to enormous animals who could kill any one of us. But I do have to admit, Polly is very ingratiating."

He laughed. He'd been so relieved when he heard Vivian's infectious laugh bubble out when Polly had licked her hand.

"She's a wonderful horse. Everyone who rides her says she takes great care of them."

"Have you ridden her? Do you ride?" Vivian asked.

"Not Polly, but yes, sometimes. There's a horse I get on well with here—Luka—but I don't have the opportunity that often." He lowered his voice. "I learned as an adult; it was a . . . strategic move. A good skill for me to have, in the jobs I did, just like golfing."

When they were all outside, Tim beckoned Vivian to his side.

"Here." He handed her a carrot. "Walk up to Polly's head and hold this out to her."

Vivian glanced back at Malcolm—she was clearly still somewhat nervous—but she stepped forward and held out the carrot. Polly took it from her delicately and then bit down so hard, carrot pieces went flying. Vivian laughed that wonderful laugh yet again.

"She certainly likes snacks, doesn't she?" Vivian rubbed her hands together. "Something the two of us have in common."

All three of them laughed at that.

"Ms. Forest, how would you like to take a little turn around the field on Polly?" Tim asked her.

Vivian shook her head and sighed.

"I was worried that's where this was going."

Malcolm put his hand on her shoulder.

"You don't have to if you don't want to, but I promise, Polly will take good care of you. And I'll ride with you, if you want."

Vivian pursed her lips at him.

"I'm going to need a little more than that. I've spent fifty-four years getting up every morning and not getting on a horse that day. What exactly makes today the day to make a different decision than the one that's served me well for life?"

Malcolm laughed. Whether she ended up getting on the horse today or not, he was going to have fun trying to persuade her.

"You take some convincing, don't you? All right, how about this: just think of your daughter's face when you get back to Sycamore Cottage today and tell her you rode a horse."

He saw in an instant he'd landed on the winning argument.

"She's never going to believe it," Vivian said. A grin spread across her face. "I love it. Okay, fine. I'm terrified, but let's do this."

Tim put a saddle on Polly, while Malcolm walked Vivian over to introduce her to Luka. A few minutes later, they walked back to Tim.

"Now, I'll hold her; just step up on the mounting block, hold on to the reins here, slip your left leg in the stirrup, then toss your right leg over her."

Vivian looked from one of them to the other, the panic back on her face.

"Just like that? We're not going to work up to this? Don't I have to change, or get instructions about how to do it, or learn what to do with my hands and my legs or anything?"

Tim shook his head.

"All of that will come once you're on the horse. Easier to teach it that way."

Vivian turned and stared at the side of the horse. She stood like that, without saying anything, for almost a minute. Malcolm almost stepped forward to tell her she didn't have to do this if she didn't want to, but something in her body language told him to stay quiet.

"Okay," she finally said.

And then, before Malcolm could blink, she hopped up on the mounting block, slid her foot into the stirrup, swung the other leg over the horse, and sat down.

She looked down at Tim and Malcolm, pride and fear both clear on her face.

"Okay, now what? I'm on her back. What do I do next?"

Malcolm smiled up at her and let Tim answer.

"Good work. Now, loosen your grip. Just relax a little." Her hands were taut on the reins. Luckily, Polly didn't protest. With what looked like great effort, she relaxed them.

"Good, good, just like that."

Another stable hand led Luka out, and Malcolm quickly mounted him. Vivian still looked nervous but already more comfortable than she had just a few moments ago.

"What do you say to going for a little walk around with them?" he asked. Vivian glanced into the distance and tensed up again. "Just inside the fenced area, I mean. So you can get used to this."

Vivian made a face at him.

"Do I have any choice?"

He looked straight into her eyes and nodded.

"Absolutely, you do. It's completely your choice. If you're not liking this, or if you want to stop at any time, just say the word, and we'll get you off that horse and inside to drink some tea and eat some scones as soon as possible."

Vivian's face softened.

"Okay. But . . . one question: How do I get her to walk?"

Malcolm grinned.

"Don't worry, she'll follow me and Luka. Here, just hold on, and I'll show you." Malcolm nudged Luka with his knees, and he walked a few steps, and Polly followed them. "See? How was that?"

Vivian smiled, but she still looked nervous.

"That was okay." She looked down at Tim. "Did that look okay?"

Tim stepped back and nodded.

"Well done. Polly likes having you up there, I can tell."

When they got a few lengths away, Malcolm turned to Vivian.

"He's not just saying that, you know. He really can tell. And if he thought the horse was unhappy with you on her, you would have been off that horse within seconds. Tim is a very keen judge of character."

Vivian nodded. He wasn't sure if she believed him or not, but he was telling the truth. Her eyes didn't budge from the back of Polly's head, and he could tell it was taking a tremendous effort for her not to hold on tightly to the reins.

"It's okay to look around, you know," he said.

She glanced quickly at him and then back at the horse.

"It just feels like if I look in any other direction, when we're moving like this, I'll go off-balance and fall off." She turned her head again and looked at him for longer this time. "I'm sure that sounds ridiculous to you."

He shook his head. He was so pleased she was enjoying herself—despite her fear—that nothing she said would have sounded ridiculous to him.

"I can definitely see how you'd feel that way, but you have a really good seat—how do you have such great posture, anyway?"

She laughed.

"Ballet lessons as a kid. I only took them for a few years, but the posture stuff all stuck with me. And I have a job where I walk around and talk to people a lot; it helps not to be hunched over a computer all day like so many people are."

He had to fight not to hunch over his computer—or his phone—on a daily basis.

"See, you already have a natural advantage for riding. No wonder you're so good at this. Do you want to learn a little bit more?"

She took a deep breath and nodded.

"Sure, okay."

He thought for a second.

"What would you rather do, go faster—not much faster, mind you—or learn more about how to use the reins?"

"Go faster," she said right away. Then she laughed. "I don't know why I said that; the idea of going faster makes me so nervous, but it also feels like the more fun choice. And I'm already up here. I might as well do it."

"Are you sure?" he asked.

She shook her head.

"Of course I'm not sure. I'm not sure about any of this, but let's do it anyway."

He grinned and relaxed his grip on Luka's reins and nudged him again. The horse began to trot, and Polly followed his lead.

"Now, the thing to get used to here isn't so much the speed, because we really aren't going that much faster, but it's the different way you feel in the saddle. It's a lot more bouncing, and it takes a little while for you to bounce in sync with the horse. It's easier to just relax into it. You'll get into the rhythm soon."

Vivian glared at him.

"You know, *that* is a thing it would have been really useful to tell me before my poor butt started getting jolted like this. No wonder riding makes people sore. I'm going to have bruises everywhere."

He reached out to her, but she was too far away to touch.

"I'm sorry, we can go back to walking again."

She shook her head and continued to bump up and down on her horse.

"No, now I have to figure this trotting thing out. I can't start it and then give up. Plus, I can't be accused of not having rhythm!"

He laughed.

"Horseback riding is sort of like dancing, when you think about it. Every partner is different; it's always better if the two of you work together."

She turned to him and opened her mouth, then closed it.

"What were you about to say, Ms. Forest?" He couldn't hold back his grin.

"Nothing." She looked straight ahead, but he could see the smile on her face. "Nothing at all."

They grinned at each other for a moment.

"Now, just remember, relax into Polly's rhythm here."

After a minute or so, she turned to him with a huge smile on her face.

"That's it! I got it!"

He watched her and Polly ride next to him and Luka.

"You got it!"

She reached down and patted the side of the horse.

It made him happy to see her smile like this as they rode

together. He'd really wanted her to enjoy this trip to the stables—he'd hatched this plan to get her to ride on a whim, and he was so pleased it had been successful.

They continued to ride around the perimeter of the pasture for the next twenty minutes until he saw Vivian shiver. The sun was about to set, and it was getting even colder out.

"I think it's time to go back in," he said.

She shook her head.

"Just one more round?"

He laughed.

"An hour ago you absolutely did not want to ride a horse. Now you want just one more time around? But I saw you shiver just now. I think we need to take you inside and get some hot tea—or maybe a hot toddy."

They turned their horses and rode back toward Tim.

"Oh, hey, Malcolm?" Vivian had an odd look on her face. "One quick question I forgot to ask: How do I make her stop?"

Right, right, he hadn't mentioned that.

"A gentle pull on the reins should slow her down, and a rough one should stop her. But she'll stop when we get near Tim anyway."

Polly slowed down almost immediately, and just as they got abreast with Tim, she stopped.

"Well done, Ms. Forest," Tim said as he helped her down from the horse. "You and Polly got very comfortable together; good to see that."

"Thank you so much for your help, Tim," she said. She patted Polly on the side again, and the horse turned to nuzzle her hand. "We had a very good time together, didn't we, girl?"

"I hope you can come back and see us before you return to America," Tim said.

Vivian glanced at Malcolm, then looked away.

"I hope so, too, but if that doesn't end up happening, please know that I had a wonderful time." She laughed. "My friends are going to die when they hear this. Let alone my daughter!"

Vivian shook Tim's hand, and she and Malcolm turned to leave the stables. She still couldn't believe she'd ridden a horse. Sure, she'd ridden it slowly, but she'd actually been on horseback. Ridiculous.

She couldn't wait to tell Maddie.

She could feel the smile still on her face as she walked next to Malcolm. When Tim had said that thing about her coming again, she'd wanted to ask Malcolm if he would bring her back, but she'd stopped herself. She was having a great time hanging out and flirting with this tall, plummy-voiced chocolate bar, but he had a very important job, and must have his own family to spend time with during the holidays. She didn't want to impose on him more than she already had.

What was he even doing to celebrate Christmas, anyway? Where was his family? They'd talked a bit about his nephew and sister but no one else. Was Malcolm going to leave Sandringham soon to go to his family?

Wait. Was he married?

She turned to ask him.

"Are you . . . ?"

Her voice trailed away. Right in front of them was a short, elderly woman, wearing a very practical mackintosh, a black purse hanging off her elbow, and a scarf over her head.

"Your Majesty." Malcolm bowed. "May I introduce Vivian Forest? She's a guest at Sycamore Cottage."

Without thinking about it, Vivian dropped into a quick curtsy.

"Ms. Forest, a pleasure. I saw you out there earlier on Polly. Excellent seat."

Vivian swallowed hard.

"Thank you, Your Majesty." What in God's name was happening to her? Did she actually just address someone as "Your Majesty" for real? "I had a lovely time riding her; she's a beautiful horse."

The Queen nodded.

"She is indeed." She turned to Malcolm. "Thank you for your note; we can discuss it in our meeting tomorrow morning."

Malcolm nodded again.

"Thank you, ma'am."

The Queen lifted a hand in farewell and walked ahead of them out of the stables, back toward Sandringham House.

Vivian hadn't realized she was standing still and staring straight in front of her until Malcolm slipped his arm through hers and turned to lead her back toward Sycamore Cottage. They didn't speak a word to each other until they were well out of the stables.

"After all your scorn of the monarchy and making fun of people who bow and curtsy to them, who was it I saw drop into an impeccable curtsy just now?" Malcolm had an enormous grin on his face.

Vivian threw her hands in the air.

"I didn't do it on purpose, okay? It just happened! It's not every day in my life a queen just lands in my path as I'm walking out of a stable! I saw you bow and I just lost my mind!"

He shook his head.

"So many revolutionary ideals that came crashing to a halt!"

The Queen. She had really met *the Queen*. Vivian laughed out loud.

"I cannot believe that just happened!" She turned to Malcolm. "Did you know she was going to be there?"

Had he brought her to the stables both to try to get her to ride a horse and to "accidentally" get her to meet the Queen?

"I didn't," he said. "But you should be honored by her compliment on your seat; she would never say that if it wasn't true."

Not only had she *met* the Queen, but the Queen had given her a genuine compliment on her horseback riding?

She'd definitely fallen down a rabbit hole. None of this felt real.

She stopped to look around.

"What a strange place this is," she said.

Malcolm followed her glance, from Sandringham House

to the stables to Sycamore Cottage to some of the other buildings in the distance.

"Quite," he said.

She laughed out loud.

"Maddie isn't going to believe this," she said. "I never even thought I might meet the Queen while I was here—I thought there was no way someone like me would be allowed near her. I did sort of hope . . ." She stopped herself. She didn't need to admit that.

Malcolm touched her elbow.

"No, you can't stop like that. What did you 'sort of hope'?"

She shouldn't have started this, but now she'd have to finish.

"This is silly, so please don't judge me for it. But I did ask Maddie if we'd get to see some tiaras. I've never seen one in real life before. A real one, I mean." She sighed. "But Maddie said no. Apparently, they don't wear them that often."

Malcolm smiled at her and took her arm again.

"No judgment here. The jewels of the royal family are really something to see in person. Some of them come out for the holidays, but your daughter was right; not the tiaras."

They turned back toward Sycamore Cottage. Vivian suddenly remembered what she'd been about to ask Malcolm when they'd been interrupted by the Queen.

"How much longer are you at Sandringham? What are your plans for Christmas? Is your family expecting you?"

He shrugged.

"The timing all depends on work, but I'll spend Christmas at my sister's."

She had to just ask it. She was dying to know.

"Just you? Are you married?"

He looked taken aback for a moment but smiled at her.

"No, not anymore. I've been divorced for . . . almost six years now." His eyes crinkled at her. "And you?"

She forgot that he might wonder that.

"Oh goodness, no. I've been divorced for almost thirty years now!"

They both laughed.

"What does your family usually do for Christmas?" he asked. "I assume you would be with your family if you weren't here?"

She nodded.

"I would be—we all go over to my aunt's house. My aunt and cousins do a lot of the cooking, but everyone is in charge of something. I'm sure I'll be homesick on Christmas Day, but I'm actually pretty excited not to have the same food and watch the same sports as I have all of my life. It'll be fun to experience something different."

She was actually looking forward to trying all of the English Christmas foods she'd only read about in books. She really hoped Julia made mince pie—she had no idea what mince pie was even made of, but she wanted to try it.

"What will you and your daughter do for Christmas here?" he asked.

"For Christmas Eve, I think Julia is going to make a big

meal for all of the staff at Sycamore Cottage, and though the Duke and Duchess have treated me and Maddie like guests, that includes us. I'm looking forward to that. I'm sure her cooking will be delicious. The Duke and Duchess will both be at Sandringham House that night, and again on Christmas morning and for lunch. So I think on Christmas Day, Maddie and I will just have a relaxing and low-key day, which is very different from our Christmases with our family at home, so that will be a nice change. We leave for London the next morning to spend a few days there before flying back to California."

They walked up to Sycamore Cottage, and he released her arm right before they got to the front door.

"Thank you for this afternoon," he said.

She smiled at him.

"Oh no, thank you! I had a wonderful time."

He took a step back as James opened the front door.

"As did I. Have a good evening."

When Vivian walked inside, it was to find her daughter looking at her with a huge grin on her face.

"Okay, Mom. I need more details about what's going on between you and that *very* attractive man."

Vivian smiled and shook her head.

"I can't imagine what you mean."

Maddie laughed out loud.

"Oh really? I saw you two walking up here, arm in arm. Come on. Don't worry, the Duke is out somewhere, and the Duchess is upstairs. You won't have an audience."

Okay, fine, she had to tell her daughter *something*.

"I'll admit that he is a very attractive man. But I promise, nothing is going on there. I have a feeling he doesn't see that many black people during the course of his job, which is probably why he gave me the tour of Sandringham yesterday. When we were there, we saw the stables out of a window, and I said something about them, so today we went to the stables. But that's all—I probably won't even see him again before we leave."

Though . . . she needed to find a way to ensure that part wasn't true.

She grinned at Maddie.

"But that's not important—listen to what happened when we were at the stables: I met the Queen!"

Maddie almost dropped her wineglass.

"WHAT? The Queen? The ACTUAL Queen? Tell me everything."

"Not only did I meet her, she gave me a compliment! She saw me riding—"

"Wait, WHAT?" Maddie stared at her. Vivian steered her daughter into the sitting room so she could put that glass of wine down before she really dropped it. "You rode a horse? What is going on?"

Vivian laughed.

"Get me some of that wine, and I'll tell you the whole story. Just wait until I tell Aunt Jo. She's going to lose it."

Vivian walked up the stairs an hour later. She wondered if she'd see Malcolm again. She hadn't wanted to be direct about wanting to see him again when they said good-bye, so she'd said nothing.

Wait. Why hadn't she wanted to be direct? What possible benefit was there for her in not being direct? Here she was, on vacation in England, and there was this attractive man—why shouldn't she tell him what she wanted? All he could say was no. So what? Plenty of people had said no to her in her life. What would it matter if he did?

When Vivian walked into her room, her eyes landed on Malcolm's letter of the morning on top of the bureau in the corner, and she smiled.

She suddenly knew what to do.

Chapter Five

When Malcolm walked into Sandringham House the next morning, the normally calm building was bustling in preparation for the upcoming royal family Christmas festivities. He dodged around the rest of the staff and the many, many Christmas decorations as he made his way up to his small office. This house had so many Christmas trees he'd lost count.

When he got to his office, he picked up his phone and called over to the prime minister's office, to see if there was any kind of concrete plan. Fifteen minutes later, he hung up the phone with a long sigh. Why had he even bothered calling? No one over there seemed to know anything. At least he knew that if they got to Christmas Eve without any decision, he wouldn't have to worry about this again until early January. There would be a real riot if the whole government had to cancel their holidays.

Just then, a footman knocked on his open door.

"This was just delivered for you, sir." The footman handed him a folded piece of paper, and he flipped it open.

Mr. Hudson,

Would you do me the honor of gracing Sycamore Cottage with the pleasure of your company on the evening of Christmas Eve? Ms. Madeleine Forest, Julia Pepper, James Dogal, the rest of the Sycamore Cottage staff, and I would all be delighted for you to join our Christmas Eve festivities.

Kind regards,
Vivian Forest

He read her note twice and realized how big the smile was on his face. He immediately reached for his notepad.

Ms. Forest,

I accept your invitation with pleasure. Would you do me the honour of riding with me again tomorrow? This time, we could even go outside the fences, if that idea is acceptable to you.

Sincerely,
Malcolm Hudson

He buzzed for someone to deliver his letter to Sycamore Cottage.

When he got back to his office after his meeting with the Queen, another note was on his desk.

Mr. Hudson,

Nothing would delight me more than to further my acquaintance with Polly. I look forward to welcoming you tomorrow at 2 p.m., if that time is acceptable to you. I cannot guarantee it, but there may be scones here to greet you.

Kind regards,
Vivian Forest

He grinned down at the paper. Vivian had asked him the day before if he was married, and this minor interaction with her made him so relieved he wasn't anymore. His ex-wife had always been irritated with him when he dropped his work facade to joke around with Miles, or to attempt to joke around with her. She certainly never would have written him notes like this, which he could tell amused both him and Vivian very much.

As he reached for stationery to write Vivian back, his phone lit up with a text from his nephew.

When do you get back to London? Mum is
driving me batty. I wanted to escape and hide

at your flat but I didn't know if you were going
to be there. Plus I can't wait to tell you my
news!

Malcolm laughed. Like a true teenager, Miles only texted him when he needed something from him.

He felt a pang of guilt that he'd just decided not to go back to London until Christmas Day so he could have Christmas Eve dinner with Vivian. He quickly brushed the guilt away. Miles could deal with his mother, and his news would keep, whatever it was.

Ms. Forest,

Scones would be very welcome, and if you please, could you save me some of the sandwiches this time? Smoked salmon is my favourite, but I'll happily eat any sandwich prepared by Ms. Julia Pepper.

All my best,
Malcolm Hudson

He got another note from her less than an hour later, scrawled a response and slid it into an envelope. He reached for the phone to summon a footman again but hesitated. The staff was awfully busy today, and running notes back and forth for him to a cottage a fifteen-minute walk away really wasn't their job.

He glanced at the clock. He'd been sitting at his desk for almost four hours at this point anyway; he needed to stretch his legs.

He pulled on his coat. This one, he could deliver himself.

Vivian was curled up in the most comfortable chair in the sitting room at Sycamore Cottage, a book in her hand and a cup of tea at her elbow. Maddie and the Duchess were doing some more fittings or whatever it was they did in the Duchess's wardrobe room for hours, so she'd had all morning to relax and nap and read the book she'd been absorbed in the morning before.

But this morning, she'd barely read a single chapter. She'd sent James over to Sycamore Cottage with that letter before she'd even had coffee this morning, and had been on pins and needles as she chatted with Maddie and drank coffee and ate the ham for breakfast that British people apparently called bacon. James—bless him—had waited until after Maddie had already left the breakfast table to bring her Malcolm's next note. And ever since then the notes had flown back and forth.

It had been a while since she'd sent the last one. Was he going to write back to her? Had it been too bold of her to start sending the notes in the first place? Or—she cringed—to ask him to Christmas Eve dinner? She'd basically just asked him out, without even really knowing if he was interested in her.

And sure, he'd said yes, then he'd asked her to go riding

again, but had he done that just to be nice? People said that the British always seemed nice to Americans, but that Americans didn't understand that they were making fun of them to their faces. But Malcolm was a busy man; he wouldn't choose to spend all this time with her just to be polite.

They also said Americans were too direct for British people, and that was probably true, too—he'd seemed taken aback a number of times at her questions, like when she asked him if he was married. Was asking him to dinner too direct? Should she have just hinted around until . . . until what, exactly? Until he left Sandringham and they never saw each other again?

Cultural exchange was hard. Especially if it seemed like you both spoke the same language but really didn't.

She glanced down at her book and burst out laughing at herself. She'd been sitting in this chair for at least the past hour and hadn't read a word. What was it about Malcolm that had made her so giddy and distracted?

She knew the answer to that question: Malcolm was attractive, fascinating, and clearly interested in her as a person; that's what it was about him. She hadn't encountered a man with all three of those traits in . . . well, far too long. Most of the men she dealt with these days were men who wanted women around to take care of them, who had no interest in who the women actually were, as long as they had breasts and could cook. Some of them were men she'd known for years, who were either newly single, or newly in their sixties and had their own mortality hit them in the face, and came sniffing around her, once all the women in their thirties they tried to hit on had rejected them.

She'd even gone out on dates with a few of them, because she'd been lonely, and hell, a woman had needs. But she got so tired of them monologuing throughout an entire dinner about themselves and their jobs and their new cars and how important and successful they were, et cetera, et cetera, and not asking a single damn question about her. The night she'd gotten a promotion a few years back, she had a third date with a man she'd previously mostly liked, and when she'd sat down and told him about it, he said, "That's nice," and then charged right into a story about the book he wanted to write someday. She'd wanted to throw her glass of wine in his lap and leave, but instead she just ordered the most expensive food on the menu, didn't even pretend to reach for her wallet when the check came, and never responded to his calls again. She learned from one of her patients that was called "ghosting"—that man had deserved to be haunted, as far as she was concerned.

So it was refreshing for a man to ask her questions about herself, and actually listen to her answers. And to hell with it: she only had a few days left in England, so she was going to let herself be excited as much as she wanted to be.

She'd hesitated to invite Malcolm to Christmas Eve dinner for only one real reason: Maddie. She and Malcolm weren't dating, but they were both clearly attracted to each other, and she knew Maddie would sense that and get all in her mother's business about it. But she was an expert at deflecting Maddie; she could handle this. Not even Maddie would think there was any future with a man who lived thousands of miles away. Plus, she was on vacation, for God's sake—everyone did something a little out of character on vacation, didn't they?

Anyway, whether or not she got another note back from Malcolm today, she was going to see him and go riding with him again tomorrow, then he was going to come to dinner at Sycamore Cottage for Christmas Eve the next day, and she had all of that to look forward to. And after that, she and Maddie had a cozy Christmas Day planned, then they would head to London for a few days before they had to fly home, and she would get to walk by Buckingham Palace and know she'd met the Queen a few days before. She smiled. This vacation was unlike any she'd ever had before.

She glanced at her watch. Julia had said she'd have lunch ready at one, and it was almost that time. She should make her way into the kitchen.

She stood up and winced. How was it that she'd spent less than an hour on that horse, but her whole body hurt? Could she really handle doing it again?

She went through the front hallway on her way to the kitchen, and just as she walked by, James opened the front door.

"James, hello," a now-familiar voice said. "I have a note for Ms. Vivian Forest, if you would be so kind as to—"

Vivian stepped forward.

"Ms. Vivian Forest is right here," she said. Had he been delivering the notes to her all morning? She assumed he'd had someone else deliver the notes, but she had no real idea.

"Oh!" he said. He looked adorably confused to see her stand-ing behind James. She smiled at him, and he smiled back.

Oh God, did she look okay? She'd obviously gotten dressed in actual clothes and put on makeup this morning; no matter how nice the Duke and Duchess were, and how much they told her to treat this house as if it was her own, she was still staying in a house with royalty, for God's sake. She couldn't walk around braless and without her hair done in a house with royalty. But she hadn't gotten dressed and put makeup on with the intention of seeing Malcolm right away. And after her ac-cidental jet lag–induced nap, she had no idea what her hair looked like. Plus, she definitely didn't have lipstick on.

James opened the front door wider and stepped back, so Malcolm had no choice but to come inside.

"I believe that's for me," Vivian said, and reached out for the note in his hand.

James faded away into the back of the house.

Malcolm handed the note to her.

"It is," he said. "I'm sorry to disturb you. If you're in the middle of something, I can just . . ."

Vivian shook her head.

"No, I wasn't, but if you're busy, I can . . ."

She stopped, only because she didn't know what the end of that sentence was supposed to be. She could what? Go hide away in another room and read her letter and smile at it in-stead of smiling at him? That's what she would have done if James had brought her the letter, but now that Malcolm was here in person, she wanted to see him, not just his handwriting on the page.

"Oh no, I have some time, if you wanted to . . ." He also trailed off just like she had.

They looked at each other and smiled, and she made a quick decision.

"I'm just about to have lunch. Would you like to join me?" she asked. "Julia made some sort of soup, and I'm sure it'll be delicious." There, she'd done it again. If he was too busy or just didn't want to, he could say no, but she didn't want him to walk back to his tiny office at the top of that enormous house; she wanted him with her.

He bit his lip. He was going to say no, wasn't he?

"As charming as Julia's soup sounds, I have a better idea. You haven't seen much of the area yet, other than the Sandringham Estate. Would you like to go into town for lunch?" He looked at his watch. "I have a phone call at two thirty, so we can't linger too long, and maybe you'd rather stay here, but . . ."

She shook her head.

"I'll get my purse and my coat."

She ran up two flights of stairs to her bedroom, her book under her arm and Malcolm's note gripped between her fingers. The first thing she did when she got into her bedroom was look at herself in the mirror. Thank God, all of her frenzied feelings of the morning hadn't made her hair as disheveled as her emotions felt. Then she opened Malcolm's note, read it, and laughed. She tucked it into the pocket of her suitcase where she'd put the rest of his notes, and put some lipstick on.

Maddie would tease her forever if she knew she was going out with Malcolm again. Vivian hadn't told her yet that she'd invited Malcolm for Christmas Eve dinner, even though she had cleared it with Julia first. She'd almost held back from inviting him to dinner; she knew her daughter would never let her live it down.

But, as her mother always used to say, life is short. Between her sister's illness, her work colleague who had died suddenly the year before, and other crises that had hit her friends and family members, that maxim resonated a lot with her after the past few years. It was one of the reasons she'd given in and had come on this trip with Maddie. You never knew what could happen. She'd gotten the chance to flirt some more with an attractive British man. She wasn't going to let this slip through her fingers.

Malcolm was still alone in the front hallway, thank goodness. James appeared with her coat, just as she was about to look around for him. She was pretty certain that man was magic.

"Thank you, James," she said. Malcolm took her coat from James and helped her slip it on. She thanked him, like this was a normal and everyday thing for a man to do and not something making her swoon inside.

"Thank you." She turned to the front door and then back around with a start. "Oh no, I need to apologize to Julia for missing lunch. Do you want to wait for me here?"

Malcolm shook his head.

"I'll come with you. We can go out through the kitchen door."

Vivian led Malcolm through the house to the kitchen and came upon Julia stirring something in a big red pot. It smelled delicious.

Before she could say anything to Julia, Malcolm stepped in front of her.

"Julia, please forgive me, but I'm stealing Vivian here away for lunch. I hope it doesn't ruin your plan."

Julia looked up at them and shook her head.

"First you come and steal all of my scones, then you steal my guest away. What are you going to do next?" She waved them out the door. "No hard feelings, this time."

Vivian looked at Julia. She still felt guilty for bailing on her for lunch, when they'd discussed the soup just this morning.

"I'm so sorry, Julia. I don't want you to think . . ."

Julia brushed her apologies away.

"Go, and have a great time, and come back and tell me how much better my food is." She grinned at Malcolm. "Glad you can join us for Christmas Eve. Unfortunately, there are no scones on the menu."

Malcolm opened the back door for Vivian.

"I take that as a personal slight. I hope you realize that." Julia's laughter rang out at them as they walked out the back door.

Malcolm put his hand on her back to guide her to the right

when they got outside. She felt that small touch throughout her body.

"This is the easiest way to get to my car."

It was colder than the day before; Malcolm put his hands in his pockets and hunched against the cold. She really couldn't hold out against the hat any longer, could she? She took a few bobby pins out of her coat pocket and twisted and pinned her hair into a messy bun at the nape of her neck. With a sigh, she pulled her hat on.

"How close is the town?" she asked.

"Just about ten minutes away. It's an easier commute than when the Queen is in London or Windsor, that's for sure. The traffic from here to there—especially at this time of year—is almost nonexistent."

"Commute?" She realized she hadn't thought of that. "Where do you stay when you're working out of Sandringham?"

He glanced down at her, and a smile spread over his face. Was he smiling because of how she looked in her hat? She knew she shouldn't have put this thing on.

"At a nearby hotel," he said. "I've stayed in one of the rooms in the house once before, and never again. That was the most uncomfortable few days in my life."

She laughed at the look of reminiscent horror on his face.

"Why? What was so terrible about it?"

He held up a hand.

"You feel how cold it is right here, outside, walking into the wind? That's how cold it is inside that house at night when you're trying to sleep. It was built in the 1800s, there's no central heating, and every window somehow has at least four drafts in it, even though that doesn't make sense. I knew all of that going in, of course, but I didn't understand what it would feel like. I even brought an extra blanket, but I should have brought an entire tauntaun to cut open and get in the middle of."

When she laughed, he shook his head.

"Oh, I'm not done. It's worse during the holidays, because the whole family comes for Christmas, so any staff who has to be up here—and even some of the family members—get assigned to old servants' quarters. And one thing that people really did not care about when building homes in the 1800s was the comfort of their servants." He led her into a small parking lot. "Now, I stay in a nice, small hotel in town, where the woman who owns it loves the royal family and therefore treats me with an overwhelming amount of respect because I work for the Queen. Normally, I hate that, but for a hotel, it's ideal. I'm never bothered when I don't want to be, the temperature in my room is always perfect, and I can get meals whenever I want, which is all I need from a hotel."

He unlocked his car and smiled at her.

"How are you enjoying your stay at Sycamore Cottage? Other than Julia's delicious food, of course."

She laughed.

"You can't separate those two things—I'm sure I'll be talking about Julia's delicious food for years to come. She made ham and cheese croissants for breakfast today—just because! I had one warm out of the oven." She could still taste that first flaky, savory, buttery bite. "But everything has been lovely— the Duke and Duchess are very kind, and it's a quite comfortable house. If only I didn't have jet lag, this trip would be perfect so far." She laughed. "But at least I can text my family and friends back home in the middle of the night."

When they got into his car, he flicked on the heated seats on her side.

"Ah, but you're on vacation," he said. "You can supplement those middle-of-the-night wake-ups with a nice afternoon nap. I'll get you back just in time for it."

She grinned at him.

"First the nap, then more tea and more of Julia's treats—I could get used to this kind of vacation."

Malcolm drove off the estate and toward the town. He suddenly realized he was actually alone with Vivian for the first time—every other time he'd seen her, they'd been surrounded by the many visible and invisible people who lived and worked on the Sandringham Estate. But now they were off the estate and alone in his car. It felt freeing.

"There's a pub right in town that's perfect on a chilly day like today, if that's okay with you."

She nodded.

"That sounds wonderful. Though I may need a translator. You have all sorts of food here in England that I've never heard of in California."

He laughed.

"Separated by a common language indeed," he said. "But yes, I'll be happy to translate for you if needed, though there will absolutely be some recognizable things like fish and chips and chicken pie on the menu."

She turned to him and pursed her lips together.

"Chicken . . . pot pie?"

He bit his lip.

"Maybe not so recognizable after all!"

She took her gloves off and tucked them into her pocket.

"Well, this could be a very educational lunch."

They walked into the pub a few minutes later and were quickly seated at a small, round table by the fire. The chairs were positioned close to each other, both facing the fire. The table was just snug enough that their arms almost touched.

Vivian took off that knit hat that had made him smile and tucked it into her purse. Her hair went every which way; he wished he knew her well enough that he could brush it back for her. She quickly unpinned her bun and smoothed her hair down with her hands before she picked up the menu.

"Hmm, okay, yes, there are certainly some things I know on this menu. Fish and chips—you promised that, and you were right. Sandwiches—I know what those are, and those also come with chips, which I imagine are of the 'fish and' variety, and not the 'bag of' variety that we have in America.

Ooh, and shepherd's pie—that sounds like a very cozy-by-the-fire kind of December meal."

Her eyes twinkled at him over the menu. He smiled back at her and congratulated himself for having the good sense to ask her out to lunch.

"I've had the shepherd's pie here, and it's delicious," he said.

She wasn't done.

"But then you have the aforementioned chicken pie—that could be anything, honestly. And there are pasties, which . . ." She pressed her lips together and looked up at him with a sly look on her face. "Well, I don't think of food when I hear that word, let's just put it that way."

He tilted his head.

"What in God's name do Americans . . . ?"

She went on.

"Scotch eggs—I think I know what those are, but I have no idea what a ploughman's board is. Mushy peas—does that literally mean you take some peas and mash them like potatoes? Is that like baby food? And . . . oh yes . . . it's here! Bubble and squeak. I thought that was one of those things that only showed up in books that got exported to America as a joke the entire United Kingdom played on Americans, but it's really on the menu!"

He put his hand down on the table.

"Okay, look. I know you're having your fun about our food, but you have a great deal of odd food where you come from, too. I've seen what you people do with sweet potatoes for your Thanksgiving dinners—how did marshmallows get there?"

She let out that infectious chuckle of hers again.

"No, you're right, that's disgusting, but I swear, we don't do that in my family!"

They grinned at each other.

He knew why he liked Vivian so much now. Or, at least, one of the reasons. It was because she talked nonsense with him in a way no one else did. Everyone else (well, everyone except for his nephew) wanted him to be serious and sober and thoughtful. Sure, of course, he joked around with his mates, and he went out for drinks with his old friends from his Parliament and consulting days, but they all still groused about work, or took the piss out of one another, or bragged about themselves in that way where they tried to pretend they weren't bragging, but everyone at the table knew they were.

Vivian joked around with him like this about food, and wrote nonsense letters back and forth with him—whether to humor him, or because she enjoyed it, he didn't know, but he suspected some of both. Most of all, he felt so relaxed around her, like he could be himself—not the Queen's private secretary, Malcolm Hudson, but really himself.

Their waitress came back over and asked them if they were ready to order. Vivian ordered the shepherd's pie, he ordered the chicken pie—with a wink at her—and they both ordered pints of beer.

"So, you said this is your first trip to the U.K., but do you do much traveling elsewhere?" he asked.

She shook her head.

"I wish I did. I always learn so much when I travel, no matter where I go. But no, I spent years as a single mom and never had the ability to travel much. Even after Maddie was grown up and I could take the time"—she shrugged—"I don't know, I think I somehow thought of travel—especially international travel—as one of those things other people did, you know? I did go on one trip with a bunch of my girlfriends over ten years ago now, and I had so much fun. Plus, my sister has had a lot of health problems in the past few years, and I haven't wanted to leave her."

"She's on the mend, I presume, since you're here?" he asked.

She nodded.

"She is, thank God." She laughed. "She told me I wasn't allowed to keep texting to check in on her, because I need this break, but it's hard. I'm not used to relaxing."

He leaned back.

"Then you should travel more often," he said.

The waitress brought them their beer, and Vivian thanked her.

"I wish I could," she said. "But I found out a few weeks ago that I might be moving into a new job; my boss is retiring, and he wants me to be the one to take his job. It's not guaranteed, I still have to apply for it, but his support has a lot of weight."

"Congratulations," he said. "Will you accept it if it's offered?"

She looked surprised at the question.

"Oh, of course. It's a huge vote of confidence in me, and I'm so grateful for it. And I'm so glad I'll be able to serve as an example and mentor to the younger black women in my field.

It does mean I'll be working a lot more, though, and doing very different work. One of the things I love about my job is all of the direct work I do with patients, and I won't be doing that nearly as much . . . or maybe not at all." She sighed, then smiled. "But we'll see—maybe in a few years once I've settled into this job, I can do more traveling."

She took a sip of beer and changed the subject.

"Is your family upset that you won't be back to London until Christmas Day?"

He laughed.

"Miles is, at least, but only because my sister is driving him up a wall. You see, he's spending this year before he goes off to Oxford living at home and taking a series of art classes. Sarah was never a fan of that idea, to put it mildly. I had to help talk her into it, and one compromise I got Miles to make was to live at home for the year. And Miles deserves this; he's always had exceptional grades, and he got excellent A levels . . ." He saw the confused look on her face and backtracked. "Right, I forget, that means nothing to Americans. A levels are the exams students take here in what you would call high school—they're in all different subjects, and they are crucial for university admissions."

She lifted her glass to him before she took another sip.

"Good job, Miles. And I'm impressed you got them both to compromise like that."

Malcolm smiled.

"It wasn't too difficult. Miles has loved art since he was small, and he had his heart set on spending a year really diving into it. And when he got into Oxford and they agreed to let him start next year, that calmed Sarah down some. He loves painting so much, and had always wanted to be able to have more dedicated time than just a month or so in the summer to work on it."

She smiled at him.

"You're very proud of him, aren't you?"

Was it that obvious? This woman was far too easy to talk to; it was dangerous.

"I'm sorry, was I bragging? I didn't mean to. I just—"

She laughed and shook her head.

"Brag away. I brag about Maddie all the time." She leaned back against her chair. "He seems like a good kid."

He nodded.

"He is. We spend a lot of time together—he sometimes uses my flat as a refuge from home, and I take him on fishing trips once or twice a year. Stuff like that."

He smiled when he thought of their last fishing trip, early the previous summer. Miles had made him laugh so hard he'd almost fallen into the water.

"But you were saying, Miles and your sister?" she prompted him.

He took a sip of his drink.

"Right. The two of them have always had friction, and even though Sarah wanted him to live at home this year, I think it's making their relationship worse." He shook his head. "He keeps hinting at a surprise he has to tell me about at Christmas, and if it's that he's planning to move in with his girlfriend,

Sarah is going to explode. I never understand why she gives him so much hell; he's a teenage boy, and he's a good kid."

Vivian touched his arm.

"I'm sure he is, but didn't you say his father died when he was young? I know you've helped out, but being a single mom is tough; your sister likely has a lot of worries and burdens she doesn't share with you."

He had helped Sarah out a lot, but being an uncle was a lot different than being a father, he knew that.

"That's probably true. You and Maddie have ended up with a good relationship, it seems?"

She nodded.

"We have, but the teenage years were rough. The mouth on that girl! We fought all the time." She laughed. "It's funny when I think about it now, but oof, the years between when she was thirteen and sixteen I fantasized about running away from home a few times a week. But now we're very close, and I'm really glad I came on this trip with her."

He put his hand on her arm. He'd been wanting to touch her since they sat down.

"Well that's good, because I'm glad you're here in England with Maddie—and me—too."

He slid his hand into hers, and she smiled at him. She brushed her thumb back and forth across the back of his hand, and he felt his whole body relax. He leaned in closer to her. He could smell her perfume now. He liked that he'd never smelled it before now, that only people who got this close to her could smell it.

"Malcolm, I—"

"Shepherd's pie is just what you need on a day like today." The waitress appeared and set a plate down in front of Vivian. Malcolm's chicken pie with a side of mushy peas followed suit. They quickly released each other's hands. Malcolm looked down at his food. What had Vivian been about to say?

"Do you need another pint, ma'am? Sir?"

They both shook their heads and picked up their forks.

"Well, I'm right here if you do. Just give me a wave."

Vivian took a bite of her shepherd's pie. She finally looked in his direction again, though she didn't quite make eye contact.

"She's right. This was just what I needed today."

Was it just what she had needed right at that moment, though? That's not what *he* had needed right at that moment.

Instead of saying that, he took a bite of his chicken pie.

"I'm glad you like it," he said. "If you want to try my chicken pie—not chicken pot pie, mind you—you're welcome to take a bite."

She cast her eyes over his plate and then looked up at him with pursed lips.

"I do have to admit that doesn't look like chicken pot pie, though I will say I've only ever had chicken pot pie once and didn't enjoy the experience, so I'm not an expert. But if those are the famous mushy peas . . . they look exactly like peas that got cooked for way too long and then mashed up."

He scooped some of the peas onto his fork and held them out to her.

"That is as may be, but you still have to try them. You can't leave England without sampling mushy peas; I think they hold you back at customs if you don't answer that question in the affirmative. Come on, taste them. I promise, they're better than they look."

She rolled her eyes at him but obediently opened her mouth. He smiled at her and slipped his fork inside her lips. Her lips closed over the peas, and she closed her eyes. He watched her face as she chewed, a smile dancing around her lips the whole time. After a few seconds, she opened her eyes and finally looked straight at him.

"That was disgusting," she said.

"Absolutely foul," he said. "But aren't you glad you experienced it?"

She laughed, then he laughed, then they were both laughing so hard they had to put their forks down.

Vivian finally picked her fork up and took her second bite of shepherd's pie.

"This, in contrast, is delicious, but now my stomach hurts so much from laughing I can barely eat," she said.

And she was still flustered by that moment right before the food had come. He had definitely been just about to kiss her, right here in the restaurant at lunchtime. She'd experienced men leaning over to kiss her plenty of times, and she'd even been pleased about it most of those times, so why did this not-even-a-kiss-but-almost-a-kiss have such lasting effects on her?

Maybe because up until now, she'd pretended to herself that this flirtation was just that—something light and easy and relaxed—and that the attraction she felt building for Malcolm was something neither of them would ever act on.

And now it seemed like it was a matter of when, not if, they would.

He was still sitting just as close to her, though they weren't quite touching anymore. She wanted to scoot her chair over just a tiny bit, so that her leg in her practical black pants was just against his leg, in his very nice gray wool pants. Instead, she kept eating her shepherd's pie.

He reached over with his fork and raised an eyebrow at her. She didn't like to share food, but she nodded anyway. He took a forkful of shepherd's pie.

"Yeah, that's just like I remembered it," he said. "I haven't had it here for years—usually when I'm up here I eat either on the estate or at my hotel, but it's nice to know this place is still as good as I thought."

She glanced at the clock over the fireplace when they were almost done eating.

"Did you say you had to get back for a call at two thirty? Because it's almost two."

He looked at his watch and sighed.

"One of the benefits of working over the holidays is there's never an issue when I take long lunches, but one of the downsides is I always wish they were longer." He waved at the waitress and asked for the bill.

He took her arm again when they left the pub as they

walked back to the car. It felt so natural to walk with him like this. The way their arms fit together, the way their strides matched each other's, the way her shoulder rubbed against his arm; it all felt so easy and familiar.

She'd only known this man for three days—what was she even thinking? How was it possible for her to be this relaxed when she was this close to him? She had no idea, but she was.

He opened her car door for her, and she shivered when she got into the car. He smiled at her.

"Don't worry, the heater in this car works quickly."

He started the car to drive the short distance back to the estate. She watched him as he drove with one hand lightly on the wheel, one on the gear shift, his warm brown eyes straight ahead. He had such a kind face. An attractive one, too, obviously, but part of the reason she'd been so immediately drawn to him had been the way his eyes smiled at her, the way the lines on his face crinkled when he laughed, the way he could share a joke with her without saying a word.

"I'm sorry," he said, without looking at her. "I just have to do this." He pulled over suddenly, right after a big row of trees.

She looked behind them, expecting to see a police car or something, but there was no one.

"What is it?" She turned back toward him.

He shook his head and took his seat belt off, then hers.

"I can't sit here and drive back to Sandringham with you looking at me like that without doing this." He put his arms around her, pulled her to him, and kissed her. She was so surprised, she didn't kiss back at first. He sat back and relaxed his hold on her. "I'm sorry, I thought . . . Did you not . . . ?"

She grinned, wrapped her arms around his neck, and leaned forward.

"Oh, I did."

This time, she kissed him. His kiss was just what she would have expected from him: firm, powerful, and somehow also tender. She hadn't kissed someone with this much abandon in years; she'd forgotten just how great a really good kiss could be. Finally, he pulled back and kissed her cheek on the way.

"The last thing in the whole world I want is to stop this, but—"

She nodded.

"You have to get back, I know."

He sighed and reached over to put her seat belt back on her. Why did that tiny gesture touch her heart so much? *Don't get ridiculous, V. This is just a little Christmas fling.*

He put his own seat belt on and started the car again.

"I very much hope no member of the royal family drove by and saw that, but then, I didn't care enough about it not to kiss you right here in the middle of the road." He grinned at her. "However, I did have the foresight to pull over with these trees to camouflage us."

She grinned back at him.

"I'm very glad you kissed me in the middle of the road, Malcolm," she said.

He turned into the estate.

"So am I."

A few minutes later, he dropped her off in front of Syca-more Cottage.

"I'll see you tomorrow? For riding?"

She could feel the smile spread across her face.

"See you tomorrow."

She walked up to the front door. She turned back when she got there, and he was still standing there smiling at her. James opened the door for her, and she waved to Malcolm. He waved back before he drove away.

Chapter Six

Malcolm looked over at Vivian, once again atop Polly, her seat just as perfect as when the Queen had commented on it.

He hadn't been able to stop thinking about her all evening the night before. He wanted to come back to Sycamore Cottage and pick her up after he was done with work, to take her back into town and out to dinner, and to talk to her for hours.

And he really wanted to take her back to his hotel room after that.

But she was here in England in order to spend time with her daughter, and while he knew she liked him, and was pretty certain after that kiss that she was attracted to him, he didn't know if she'd welcome him trying to monopolize all of her time.

But she was so bright and vibrant and sparkling; how could he not want to spend more time with her?

"Having fun?" he asked.

She looked around, a wide smile on her face.

"I love this," she said. "Why haven't I done this before in my life?" She laughed. "That's a silly question. I don't live a life where horseback riding is just a thing I can easily do. Not like going for a hike or to the beach or to get more avocados."

He laughed.

"We live in very different worlds."

How did this woman feel so familiar to him, despite their differences?

She patted the side of Polly's head as they rode toward the trees in the distance.

"I confess, as easy as it would be for me to do all three of those, the last one is the only one I actually do with any regularity. I don't go to the beach nearly enough, even though I'm happy whenever I'm there." A reminiscent smile spread over her face. "A while ago when I got a promotion and some back pay, Maddie and I rented a house right along the coast for a long weekend, and it was so wonderful. All we did was lie on the beach and read books and listen to the waves move in and out and eat snacks."

"That sounds heavenly," he said.

She nodded and sighed.

"It was. Granted, it's Northern California, so the beaches are often overcast, but I like the beach in any weather, even when it's gray and cloudy. We said when we left we would keep going back, maybe on her birthday, or mine, but we haven't done a weekend like that again, and it's been . . . years." She shook her head. "I don't know why. Life gets busy, with so many things that aren't actually important but feel important. And there are plenty of weekend days where I could decide to forget my to-do list, spend a few hours at the beach instead, but I've only ever done that if there's a special occasion." She looked at him and smiled again. "Life is short. I need to stop waiting for special occasions in order to treat myself."

They rode into some trees, and he grabbed her reins and slowed both of their horses to a stop. She looked at him, startled.

"Now seems like a good time for one kind of treat."

He leaned over and kissed her again. She laughed as she realized what he was about to do, but then she kissed him back. He held on to her waist so she wouldn't worry about falling, and he loved the feel of her body. She moved her hand up to his face and stroked his cheek. He wanted to stay like this forever.

Finally, his horse twitched, and they laughed and broke apart. He couldn't believe he'd kissed her twice where people could have seen them. Maybe even *had* seen them. And he couldn't bring himself to care.

"Kissing on horseback seems rather dangerous, Mr. Hudson," she said.

"Not with experienced riders like me around, Ms. Forest," he said. "I would never let anything happen to you."

She smiled as they rode on.

"I usually like to be the one who wouldn't let anything happen to me," she said. "But a little bit of danger never hurt anyone." She grinned. "Everyone at work would be shocked to hear me say that. I'm usually the cautious one."

The sunlight made her face glow. How could anyone not smile back at her when she smiled at them like that?

"Well, you're obviously very good at your job, so let's just call this different attitudes for different parts of life."

She laughed.

"How is it obvious I'm good at my job?" she asked. "I *am*, but we're over five thousand miles away from it, so how can you tell?"

He touched her hand.

"The way you can talk to everyone, the way everyone likes you—Tim, Julia, James, the Duke and Duchess—and the way you've managed to get me to talk about myself, which I try to avoid doing at all costs."

She looked down, then smiled up at him.

"Well. Thank you for that. And I'm probably so good at my job because I love it. Granted, it's really hard sometimes—as a social worker, and especially a social worker at a hospital, you see so much of the bad parts of life. But I also get to see so many good parts, or funny parts, and"—she laughed—"so many of the ridiculous parts. But I love when I know I've made a difference for a patient—connected them with services they've been desperately needing, helped fight some of their fights with the hospital or their housing or their schools for them, or done some of the heavy lifting with their families. I work with so many families who want to be good for one another, but they just don't know how, and it's wonderful when I can give them the tools to do so."

He liked how she talked about her work, with so much humor, but also kindness and warmth.

"It must get really tough, though. I'm glad you have this break."

She nodded.

"I'm glad, too. I think I needed a break more than I realized. And honestly, it feels great to be this far away from work right now, with the potential new job and all." She sighed. "It's a big deal and more money and all of that, but it means I'll get to do a lot less of the parts of my job that I love—less working directly with patients and their families, less coming up with ideas to solve problems to really help them. It'll all be a lot more global solutions for all of our patients, which is good, too, just . . ."—she sighed again—"different. And it also means I'll be working a lot more—always needing to check my email and to be available from wherever, all of that stuff I don't have to do now. So it was good to take this vacation, since it might be the last real one I have for a while."

She glanced around Sandringham with a wistful look on her face.

Malcolm suddenly had a ridiculous idea.

No, he definitely couldn't do that. It made no sense.

Or did it? Vivian said she needed more of a break, didn't

she? And Miles was always telling him he had to be more spontaneous.

He looked over at Vivian and smiled.

On the walk from the stables back to Sycamore Cottage, Malcolm reached over and took Vivian's hand. She blushed and looked away as their fingers intertwined, like if she didn't see it happening, it wouldn't be real. It had definitely been a while since she'd walked hand in hand with a man. His hand was smooth and firm, and hers felt so secure within his grasp.

"Should I bring anything for dinner tomorrow night?" he asked. "Thank you again for the invitation."

She smiled at him.

"I'm delighted that you're coming, but I'm not the person to ask that question. You should ask Julia," she said.

Was Christmas Eve going to be the last time she saw him? Probably, since he was going to leave Sandringham the next morning to go to his sister's house for Christmas.

"When do you fly back to America?" he asked.

He was apparently on her same wavelength. But she wasn't ready to think about leaving yet. This trip had been better than she'd ever imagined, and she still had days to go.

"The twenty-eighth," she said. "Maddie and I leave Sandringham the day after Christmas—Boxing Day, as I guess people really call it here—and then we're in London for a few days before we fly home."

"What would you think about staying a few extra days in London?" he asked.

"What?" She stopped and turned to him. She tried to drop his hand, but he held on. "What do you mean?"

"I mean, Maddie would fly back on the twenty-eighth as scheduled, and you would stay an extra few days. With me. Maybe through the New Year. I'm on holiday all next week, and you just said that this is your last holiday for a while, so why not make the most of it? Plus"—he looked straight at her—"I'm not ready for you to go."

Oh.

She looked down and didn't say anything.

"I'm not just flattering myself that you want to spend more time with me, too, am I?" Malcolm asked after a few seconds.

She looked back up at him.

"No, oh no, that's not it. It's just, this is so sudden. I've had a great time with you, Malcolm, but . . ."

He stepped closer to her and held more tightly to her hand.

"Didn't you just say you need to treat yourself more?" he asked.

She shook her head, but she couldn't keep the smile off her face.

"Stop throwing my words back at me," she said.

He reached up and touched her cheek.

"I can't get enough of you, Vivian Forest," he said. "Stay here in England with me, just for a few more days."

Oh wow.

"That does sound lovely," she said.

"It will be," he said.

He leaned down and kissed her again. She moved into the circle of his arms. Her body against his made her feel so warm and secure. And his hands on her body made her feel so desired.

It would be nice to spend a few days without Maddie right across the hall from her bedroom.

They walked hand in hand until he left her at the steps of Sycamore Cottage.

When she got inside, Maddie ran toward her. Oh no. With Malcolm's invitation swirling around her mind, the last thing she wanted to do was to get interrogated by her daughter.

"Oh, thank God you're here," Maddie said. "Can you come up to the dressing room? We need your help."

Vivian turned to hand her coat to James and hoped Maddie hadn't seen the relief on her face.

"Of course. What do you need?"

Maddie talked the whole way up to the second floor—or what Vivian had discovered was called the first floor here.

"We originally had six options in the running for Christmas Eve, and when I got here, the Duchess and I narrowed it down to three, and this morning we managed to narrow it down to two, but between those two, she can't decide." Maddie lowered her voice. "You know I generally have no problem ordering clients around and telling them what to wear, but this is an unusual situation, so I've tried to just do a Vivian and give her the pros and cons of both dresses and let her make the decision."

Vivian grinned. Maddie always made fun of her for her pro/con lists; it was good to know her daughter did actually listen to her.

"So, what do you need me for?" she asked.

Maddie smiled.

"She still can't decide. She likes them both so much—which thrills me, of course—but both of them need a tiny bit of alteration, and she doesn't want me to do that work for both for her to decide at the last minute, which obviously thrills me even more. So she said we should see what you think."

Vivian stopped and stared at her daughter.

"The Duchess wants my opinion?"

Maddie slid an arm through hers and pulled her along.

"She does; thank goodness I know you have good taste."

Maddie ushered Vivian into the "dressing room," which looked like an entire large bedroom devoted to the Duchess's wardrobe. She stood in the corner, in a slim, off-the-shoulder, floor-length magenta gown.

"Oh my goodness, you look wonderful," Vivian said. "Is that one of the dresses?"

The Duchess came over to her and took both of Vivian's hands in hers.

"It is, and thank you so much for coming up to give us your advice! I love both of them—your daughter did an excellent job—and I can't decide what to wear." She turned and walked back toward the window and then turned in a circle. "I want you to see them both from all sides."

Vivian walked around her.

"You look incredible in this one. I want to see you in the other one, but it'll have to be something out of this world."

The Duchess beamed at her, and Maddie raced over to unzip the dress. Vivian turned to the other side of the room and saw a row of boxes that she was sure contained jewelry. She thought of what Malcolm had said about how royal jewelry was a sight to see. God, she itched to open those boxes and peek inside. She moved away and looked at the many rows of shoes instead.

Had Malcolm really just invited her to stay in England after Maddie left? With him? She couldn't stop smiling. She'd known they were having a good time together, but she'd thought he was spending time with her mostly from a combination of boredom and loneliness. But no, he was interested in her; he wanted to spend more time with her. Not from boredom or politeness, but because he couldn't get enough of her. Wow.

"Okay, Mom. Here's the second dress."

Vivian tried to dim her smile and spun around. The Duchess was now in a sequined emerald-green gown, with a high neck and a high—but not too high—slit up the side. She spun in a circle, and glints of green light sparkled around the room. Vivian laughed.

"You absolutely have to wear that dress. I love the other dress so much—wear it to something else—but please wear this dress tomorrow night."

Maddie looked at her mom with a big smile on her face. She'd clearly picked Maddie's favorite.

The Duchess beamed at her.

"I love it, too, but are you sure about the color?"

Vivian nodded.

"Positive."

The Duchess looked at herself in the mirror and smiled.

"You're right. Yes, this one." She clasped Vivian's hands again. "Thank you so much. I think I just needed you to give me that push."

Maddie smiled and started pinning the bottom of the dress.

"I hope you've been having a good time while you've been here," the Duchess said. Vivian tried to think about how to respond to that without referring to Malcolm, but luckily, the Duchess kept talking. "Maddie said this is your first time in England; it's too bad you're leaving so soon after Christmas, but I've already given her a list of things you two should do in London."

Vivian smiled to herself.

"Yes, too bad we're leaving so soon," she said. Malcolm's idea sounded better and better the more she thought about it.

Chapter Seven

Vivian went to bed that night with a smile on her face. She woke up the next morning—Christmas Eve—in a panic. There was no way she could stay on in England with Malcolm. What had she been thinking?

First of all, she had responsibilities back at home! Sure, she was on vacation until January 3, but she needed to get her house in order, unpack, switch out her calendars, and water her plants—all the stuff she usually did after Christmas but wouldn't be able to do if she stayed in England.

Secondly, what would Maddie say? Vivian had spent decades keeping her dating life separate from her life with Maddie, and this would destroy all of that! Yes, fine, she'd invited Malcolm to Christmas Eve dinner, but she would pretend to

Maddie that was Julia's idea. There was no way she could pin an extra few days with him in London on Julia!

But most importantly, she barely knew this man! Why the hell had she even considered being alone in a foreign country with a stranger? He'd mentioned staying with him—stay with a stranger, in his home? What if he was some sort of ax murderer or something? Maybe no one would ever see her again!

No, she couldn't do this. She wouldn't stay.

Yes, that was it. When he came for dinner tonight, she'd tell him she was sorry, but there was no way she could stay; she'd had a lovely time with him, but that was it, and Merry Christmas.

Or Happy Christmas, whatever it was they said here.

Okay. Good. That was the plan.

Granted . . . she did have so much fun with him. And so what if it was just that vacation kind of fun, where they didn't really know each other or need to fit into each other's lives and nothing was at stake—it was only a few more days! They'd keep having vacation kind of fun—maybe even the better kind of fun—and then she'd go home and everything would go back to normal. Shouldn't she be in favor of having more fun in her life? Especially since she wouldn't have the opportunity to do something spontaneous like this again once she took the new job?

And he probably wasn't an ax murderer. Wouldn't she have read something about an epidemic of women in England being murdered via ax if that was the case? He did work for the Queen, after all—not that people who worked for royalty were automatically model citizens; historically, it seemed like it was very much the opposite. But she didn't really think people with those jobs got carte blanche to go around committing crimes.

She got out of bed, plucked a notebook out of her purse, and got back in bed. She needed a pro/con list, that's what she needed.

She spent ten minutes scrawling down everything she could think of on both sides of the list.

PROS	CONS
I have so much fun with him	So much to do at home
New job will mean a lot more work; last chance to do something like this for a while!	Maddie will freak out
Probably not a murderer	But he could be a murderer!
Sex! (hopefully)	Sex??? I barely know him!

She tried to come up with a fifth bullet point on either side to break the tie, but everything she thought of seemed very clearly like a secondary point to one of the eight bullet points she already had.

She shook her head and got out of bed. She needed to sit on this for a while. She should take a shower, go downstairs and drink some of Julia's delicious tea and eat some of those glorious scones she'd been stuffing herself with for days, and put this whole decision out of her mind for now.

She hadn't dated anyone in a few years, which was probably why a few kisses had gotten her so giddy about a ridiculous idea like staying with Malcolm in England after Maddie left.

Fine, that last point in the pro list was a significant one.

Maddie was busy doing final fittings with the Duchess for the Christmas Eve and Christmas Day outfits, and Julia was occupied in the kitchen, prepping for the holiday meals, so Vivian spent most of the day curled up on her favorite chair in the sitting room, reading and drinking tea and eating whatever snacks James periodically set in front of her. She hadn't had a day where she had literally nothing to do but relax in a long time, and instead of being able to take advantage of it, she kept thinking about Malcolm Hudson.

She'd sort of expected to get a note from him that day, but one didn't come. Maybe he'd changed his mind, too. Maybe he'd realized spontaneity wasn't all it was cracked up to be, and thought of all the work he had to do, and remembered he barely knew her.

Yes, that was it. He'd decided she shouldn't stay, either. Maybe they could just both pretend he'd never said anything about it the day before, so they wouldn't have to talk about it, and they'd just never speak of it tonight, then never see each other again.

Okay, well, that last part was depressing. Plus, avoiding a conversation like that wasn't really her style. She had to tell him something.

"What do you think, Mom? Isn't she stunning?"

Vivian looked up at Maddie's voice and saw the Duchess standing there in front of her in the emerald-green sequined dress. Vivian rose from her chair.

"Wow. Oh wow." Vivian walked around the Duchess to see her from all sides. Her hair was up in a loose, off-center bun, with long tendrils around her face, she had huge diamond studs in her ears, and she was wearing a diamond bracelet that probably cost twice as much money as Vivian's car.

Maybe her house.

"You look incredible," Vivian said.

"She does, doesn't she?" The Duke came into the room in his tux and smiled first at his wife, then at Maddie and Vivian. "Thank you both, for making my wife so happy."

The Duchess kissed him on the cheek.

"At first I wasn't sure about this color, but—"

"It's perfect," both Vivian and the Duke said in unison. They grinned at each other.

"Who am I to argue with these two?" the Duchess said to Maddie.

James pulled the car up to the house, and after another flurry of good-byes, they got in to drive the few minutes over to Sandringham House.

"That's our cue to get ourselves ready for dinner," Vivian said.

Maddie nudged her on their way up the stairs.

"Speaking of dinner, a little birdie told me that Malcolm Hudson is coming for dinner, too. How did that happen?"

Oops. In the aftermath of Malcolm's invitation, she'd

forgotten to find a way to mention to Maddie that he was coming tonight.

"Oh, I think Julia wanted to—"

Maddie rolled her eyes.

"Mom, stop. You wanted to spend a little more time with the very attractive and accomplished man who introduced you to the Queen. You don't need to make up a story about this on my account."

Now might be a good opportunity to tell Maddie that she was thinking about spending even more time with the very attractive and accomplished man who introduced her to the Queen.

No, she'd decided that wasn't going to happen, hadn't she?

"Plus"—Maddie grinned at her—"I heard him talking the other day when he dropped you back off here—my goodness, that accent. If I wasn't already taken, I'd swoon for it a little bit, too."

He really did have an incredible voice. It wasn't just the accent, though that was great, too. It was something about the timbre of his voice: low, but not too deep; warm and soothing, like drinking a cup of hot chocolate with a shot of whiskey.

Should his voice be a pro on her list?

No, no, be real with yourself, Vivian.

She needed to change the subject before Maddie kept talking about Malcolm.

"How did everything go with the Duchess? She looked great, but I know these past few days have been busier than you expected."

Maddie shook her head.

"I can't believe we had that dress done on time and got her out the door. This was one of the most intense styling jobs I've ever had, and while it's been a great experience, I'm looking forward to lunchtime tomorrow, when I'm all done with work and we can relax together. I'm jumping in the shower now. See you at cocktail hour!"

Vivian slowly followed Maddie up the stairs. She would have to tell Malcolm her decision tonight; she knew that. The problem was, she still had no idea what her decision would be.

Malcolm arrived at Sycamore Cottage at eight p.m. on the dot, two bottles of champagne in hand. He'd checked in with Julia, who had told him he didn't need to bring anything, but his mother had raised him to always bring something when he went to someone's house for dinner, and he had no intention of looking like a mannerless boor in front of Vivian.

"Happy Christmas, James," he said when James opened the front door.

"Happy Christmas, sir," James said. "Pleased you'll be joining us for dinner."

James had a very bland look on his face, which meant he must be aware of exactly why Malcolm was at dinner tonight. Had he seen them kissing the day before?

What was he thinking? Of course James knew exactly why Malcolm was at dinner tonight, whether or not he'd seen them kissing. James had been the one to deliver all of those notes to Vivian. People don't send notes back and forth to each other all day if they haven't at least thought about kissing each other.

"I've brought this champagne for all of us to enjoy; should I give it to you, or bring it back to Julia?"

James took the bottles out of his hands.

"I'll ask Julia when she would like it to be served. Please, come in."

James escorted him into the sitting room, which looked very different than the last time he'd been there, just a few days before. The lights were low, candles were lit everywhere, the white twinkle lights on the Christmas tree were glowing, and the fire was burning. A few other members of the Sycamore Cottage staff were already inside, including Julia. But Vivian wasn't there yet. Nor was her daughter, who he was eager to finally meet.

"Malcolm! So pleased you're joining us tonight," Julia said. She glanced over at James. "Oh, do we have you to thank for this champagne? James, would you put it in one of the ice buckets in the dining room, please? We'll have it with our first course."

Julia handed Malcolm a cocktail.

"I'm delighted I had this dinner to have fun with; I have the chance to make the dishes I always want to make for my family Christmas dinner, but am never allowed to—my family never wants to fuss with tradition. Here's the cocktail I made for all of us to start the night with."

Malcolm took a sip, and his eyes widened.

"Goodness, Julia. I feel sorry for your family that they don't have the chance to experience this drink."

She grinned at him.

"I hope that will be your feeling throughout this entire meal."

He was just about to take another sip when something occurred to him.

"Did my late addition to the party make trouble for you? If so, I apologize."

She glanced over his shoulder.

"Absolutely not. You don't think Vivian is the kind of person who wouldn't check in with me about that before she invited you, do you?"

He laughed.

"No, we've both known her only a few days, and we know that she isn't. But then, I've known you for years, and I know you're the kind of person who would always say yes to that type of request, even if it threw your entire plan into chaos."

She grinned at him.

"You know me too well, Malcolm. But I promise, that wasn't the case." She turned slightly and smiled at someone behind him. "I think you're going to want to see this."

Malcolm spun around and saw Vivian walk into the room. She had on a dark red dress, her hair was down, and her smile was dazzling. He hoped it was for him.

"You look incredible," he said in a low voice when she came over to him and Julia.

She looked away and smiled.

"Thank you. Merry Christmas." She smiled at Julia. "Merry

Christmas, Julia. The sitting room has been transformed in just the past hour. Who can I thank for this?"

Julia nodded at the corner.

"That would be James. He's excellent at decorating." She handed Vivian a cocktail. "I love your dress."

Vivian looked down at herself and smiled.

"Thank you. It's all Maddie, of course. Thank goodness for my daughter."

Malcolm touched her elbow. This was the first time he'd ever seen her not covered from head to toe against the weather. It was nice to reach out and touch her arm and feel her smooth skin, and not just her wool sweater.

"Your daughter is clearly a very talented woman," Malcolm said, "but she's lucky she has you to do her talents justice."

Malcolm heard a voice next to him.

"I'm lucky I have my mother for many reasons, but yes, that's one of them."

Malcolm turned and smiled. Maddie looked a lot like her mother.

"Maddie, this is Malcolm Hudson, the queen's private secretary." Vivian's cheeks were pink, either from the fire or from their compliments. "Malcolm, this is my daughter, Madeleine Forest."

Malcolm and Maddie shook hands and smiled at each other.

"Malcolm, thanks for entertaining my mother for the past few days while I've been so busy here," Maddie said.

She had no idea how much he'd enjoyed himself with Vivian, did she?

"The pleasure was all mine. And—"

Julia handed Maddie one of her special cocktails.

"For you, to celebrate a job well done," Julia said to Maddie. "We have a lot of good drinks in store for us tonight: we'll have champagne for our next course—some of it courtesy of Malcolm here—and some great wine with dinner, a gift from the Duke and Duchess to all of us."

Maddie took a sip of her cocktail.

"Ooh, what is in this? And don't tell me it's a secret recipe. My boyfriend is a huge cocktail fan, and he would love this— I promise I won't tell anyone else."

As Maddie teased the cocktail recipe out of Julia, Malcolm stood just as close to Vivian as he dared, and wished they were alone in this room. Or any room, really. He wanted to be able to kiss her without people around them, he wanted to be able to tell her the plans he'd made for their tiny holiday, he wanted to know for sure her smile was just for him.

"All right, I'll show you the bottle, but you have to swear you're just going to tell your boyfriend and not a single person in the United Kingdom," Julia said to Maddie.

Maddie held up her hand.

"I swear! And if it's a brand we don't have in the U.S., it would be a perfect gift to bring back to him from this trip."

Maddie and Julia walked off, presumably to go inspect the alcohol, and he and Vivian were left alone.

They weren't completely alone—James and a few other Sycamore Cottage staff and friends of staff were still milling about the sitting room, drinking Julia's special cocktail and eating the cheese straws she had in vases on the tables. But this was likely as close as they'd get, at least until the twenty-eighth.

"I'm so pleased you invited me to dinner," he said. "I wouldn't have missed you in that dress for the world."

She smoothed the dress at her hips. That quick, nervous motion made him smile.

"I'm glad you came," she said. "I have no idea what Julia has in store for us, but whatever it is, I'm sure it'll be delicious."

He nodded.

"I'm certain of that. But speaking of, I wanted to know if you had any restaurant reservation preferences for our time in London? I don't really know what kinds of food you like and don't like, other than sandwiches and scones and shepherd's pie." He grinned at her, but her smile faltered. Was she a picky eater and was scared to tell him? No matter, they could figure that out. "Oh, speaking of." He pulled a piece of paper out of his pocket. "Here's your updated itinerary."

She didn't reach for the paper.

"My updated itinerary?"

He moved closer to her so he could show it to her.

"I contacted the Duchess's private secretary, and she gave me all of the necessary information to change your flight. You'll now be on the same flight back you would have taken on the twenty-eighth; you're just leaving on the first instead." She didn't say anything, so he kept talking. "I also extended your hotel reservation; while you're welcome to stay with me in my flat, I, um, didn't want to assume."

He absolutely had wanted to assume, and he very much

hoped she would tell him there was no need for the hotel reservation when he had a perfectly fine flat in London they could stay in. But he wanted to at least give her the option.

She wasn't smiling anymore.

"Why would you make my travel arrangements without talking to me about it first?"

He didn't understand.

"We talked about it yesterday," he said. "I said we'd have a great time, and you said it did sound lovely, and . . ."

Ah. There was no "and." That was the problem. She hadn't, actually, at any point, said yes, had she?

"That didn't mean I'd decided to stay." Her mouth was a tight line. "Did you think about consulting me, before you made these arrangements?"

He took a step back.

"Does that mean you've decided not to stay in London?" She could have at least let him know in advance, before he'd shown up here to be rejected.

"What's this about you staying in London?" Maddie was suddenly at her mother's side again. Excellent, an audience. Just what he needed. At this point, he wanted to turn around and leave Sycamore Cottage and never come back.

Vivian cleared her throat.

"Oh, Malcolm suggested—since this is my first trip to England, and just to see more of London, and all—that I should stay on after you leave, but I don't think . . ."

Maddie looked from Vivian to him and back to Vivian with a big smile on her face.

"What a great idea! I was already feeling bad that you were only going to get such a short time in London; this is the best plan."

Maybe Maddie *had* been just what he'd needed?

Vivian put her hand on Maddie's arm.

"Oh, but Maddie, I need to consider . . ."

Maddie cut her off.

"You don't need to consider anything. I'm sure you've already made a great pro/con list on this, and if it was dramatically imbalanced, you wouldn't have even entertained the idea. You spend all your time working or helping Aunt Jo as it is, and you're about to start your fancy new job. You keep saying this is your last vacation for a while. You need a treat. Don't you always tell me life is too short?" She looked at Malcolm. "She's staying. Take good care of her."

Vivian sputtered.

"I've been taking care of myself for a long time. He doesn't have to take care of me."

Maddie locked eyes with Malcolm and shook her head.

"See what you've gotten yourself into?"

Just then, a gong sounded, and they all turned toward the front of the room.

"Dinner is served, everyone," James announced. "Please come into the dining room."

Malcolm offered Vivian his arm. She glanced up at him for a second and then slid her arm through his. They didn't talk as they walked into the dining room, along with the rest of the Sycamore Cottage staff and friends of staff.

They sat down at the table, and Julia poured champagne in their glasses.

"Happy Christmas Eve, all!" she said. Everyone raised their glasses, and he turned to Vivian to touch her glass with his. She looked at him with a resigned expression on her face and then sipped her champagne.

He leaned closer to her so no one else would be able to hear him.

"Vivian, I apologize. I should have checked with you before making your travel arrangements. I can easily change them again, if you don't want to stay. I don't want you to feel as if you have to."

He was glad he'd had years of work in government; he knew his face didn't reflect just how much he cared about her answer.

She looked up at him and was silent for a moment.

"No, don't. In the end, I guess I'm glad Maddie intervened. She was right." She pointed a finger at him. "You are *not* allowed to tell her that."

He laughed, and she finally—finally—smiled at him.

"I promise." He put his glass down. "But I truly am sorry; I'm not used to spontaneity, and I suppose it went to my head. Can you forgive me?"

She touched his hand.

"I appreciate the apology. And if I didn't think I could forgive you, I wouldn't stay, now would I?" She lifted her glass to him. "To spontaneity."

He laughed and looked in her eyes as their glasses clinked.

As Vivian drank her champagne, she couldn't help but see Maddie's smug smile from across the table. The next time Malcolm looked away, Vivian glared at her, but Maddie just gave her an innocent smile back.

She wasn't actually that mad at Maddie for forcing her hand about staying in England. Now that that decision was irrevocably made, she was at peace with it. Maybe even a little excited about it. No, that part she was okay with; it was the constant smirks from Maddie's side of the table that made Vivian want to send her to her room like she could when Maddie was little. This attitude must be revenge for when Vivian had known—long before Maddie had told her—about Maddie's relationship with Theo. Could she help it if she knew her daughter that well?

"Time for crackers!" Malcolm interrupted her silent fuming at her daughter and handed her the gold-wrapped cylinder from in front of her plate.

She took it from him and looked down at it. How, exactly, was she supposed to do this? Was this a thing she should unwrap? Or was there some other trick to it?

Crack!

Vivian jumped at the noise to her right. She turned, and the chauffeur and his girlfriend were giggling over their open crackers. But she still hadn't seen how they did it.

"We do it like this," Malcolm said. He picked up both of their crackers, and held them out to her. "Now, hold on." She took the other end of each cracker, and he smiled at her. "Now, I'll count to three, then we both pull. One, two, THREE."

They pulled on cue, and the crackers let off enormous bangs. Vivian gasped and then laughed. She looked over at Malcolm, who had a very satisfied expression on his face, and they both laughed even harder.

"Wait, that's not it," he said. "We have to wear our crowns." He picked up the flimsy colored-paper crowns that had fallen from inside the crackers onto the table and unfolded them. "Hmm, I think . . . the purple one for you, the pink one for me." He set the paper crown on top of her head and adjusted it carefully. "There. Beautiful."

She watched him as he put on his own ridiculous paper crown.

"This is very silly," she said. "I like it a lot."

He smiled at her.

"I like it a lot, too."

By the time they were done with the first course—pheasant cooked under a brick, which was surprisingly delicious—the entire table had on paper crowns. Julia kept bringing out more incredible food, and their compliments to her got more and more elaborate, as she poured them more and more wine. There was a mountain of tiny roast potatoes in their skins, crisp and tender Yorkshire puddings, beef Wellington, and oh, thank goodness, mince pies . . . though they didn't look like

any kind of pie she'd ever seen. For one, they were miniature—
at home, people would probably call these cookies. They were
delicious, though.

Finally, after an enormous and showstopping bûche de Noël,
the whole party headed back into the sitting room for port.

Just as Vivian was about to walk out of the dining room,
Malcolm stopped her.

"Wait, you dropped an earring," he said.

She automatically reached up to her earlobes, and sure
enough, one of her long, sparkly earrings was missing.

"Oh no!" She'd definitely had them both on earlier. They
must be somewhere in either the dining room or the sitting
room. She turned to go back to the table to look under her
chair when Malcolm stopped her.

"Is this it?" He opened his hand, and her earring was in his
palm.

"Yes! That's it, thank you." She reached for it, but instead
he held it up to her ear and gently slipped the post in. His
fingers stroked the outside of her ear, and she shivered.

"Oh. Thank you," she said again. He cupped the side of her
face and turned it toward his. "Don't you think we should . . . ?"
She looked into his eyes and suddenly couldn't remember
what she thought they should be doing other than exactly this.

He pointed up above their heads.

"Mistletoe. It's a tradition. I don't know if you do this in
America, but in Britain, we have no choice but to kiss now."

She smiled and moved closer to him.

"Well, I am in Britain, and I did say I wanted to learn about all of your Christmas traditions. Teach me this one."

He bent down to her.

"With pleasure."

He kissed her softly once, twice, then put his arm around her waist and pulled her even closer, and kissed her a third time. The third kiss started out softly, too, but when she wrapped her arms around his neck and licked his bottom lip, it quickly turned passionate. They kissed and kissed, their hands touching each other's faces, their lips and tongues dancing, their bodies snug against each other's, until they heard a discreet cough and broke apart.

Julia stood next to them, a platter of chocolates in her hands, not quite holding back a big grin.

"I see you found the mistletoe," she said. "Truffle?"

Vivian supposed she should be embarrassed, but instead she just felt proud. Getting caught making out under mistletoe, at her age! She grinned at Julia.

"Thank you, I'd love one." She reached out and picked one up with her fingers. "Malcolm?"

He, on the other hand, couldn't seem to make eye contact with Julia. She didn't know why. The whole mistletoe thing had been his idea in the first place!

"Ahem. Thank you." He took a truffle and moved out of the doorway. "After you."

Julia walked into the sitting room with the truffles, and Vivian and Malcolm followed.

"Would you like some port?" he asked her when they got back into the sitting room. "I see James pouring over there."

When she nodded, he left to get their drinks. Maddie immediately appeared at her side.

"Where did you two disappear to, hmm?" Maddie asked, that smirk still on her face.

"My earring fell out of my ear in the dining room. I had to find it," she said. Maddie's annoying grin got even bigger.

"Ah yes, you 'had to get your earring.' I know that one, too."

Vivian shook her head and tried to keep a straight face.

"I don't know what you're talking about."

Maddie giggled.

"Sorry, Mom, I'm just delighted by this." Her face turned serious. "But honestly, one of the reasons I wanted you to come on this trip was to get a break from everything at home, work and the family and everything else, and I wanted you to treat yourself a little, which we both know you never do." She glanced in Malcolm's direction. "And that over there is a real treat."

Vivian tried so hard not to grin, but she couldn't help it.

"Isn't he, though?"

They both dissolved into giggles.

Chapter Eight

Vivian woke up late on Christmas morning for the first time in years and smiled at the ceiling. She couldn't remember the last time she'd woken up on Christmas morning without having to jump out of bed and rush around—when Maddie was little, it was to get up with her, open presents, have breakfast, and head over to her mom's house. In recent years, as Vivian and her sisters had taken over a significant portion of the holiday cooking, it had been to finish up the many dishes she was cooking for Christmas dinner, and get them packed in the car, then go to her aunt's, where the whole family would be for hours.

She felt a small pang thinking about that—the family would be there all day today, and she wouldn't be with the rest of her family for the first time in her life. But it helped to remember that all she had to do today was to eventually get up from this cushy bed whenever she felt like it, put on some comfortable clothes, amble downstairs for some of Julia's delicious tea and scones, and know that no one she saw all day would comment on if she'd gained weight since Thanksgiving, or if that dress was too young for her, or if she really needed to do something different with her hair.

Maddie must have been up hours ago. Vivian grinned to herself. How the tables were turned. Maddie had to get up early on Christmas morning to help the Duchess get dressed so she would look flawless for the much-photographed walk to church, and Vivian could just recover from her night of many glasses of wine right here in bed.

That had been a good Christmas Eve party, hadn't it? The cocktails, the champagne, Julia's amazing food . . . and then, of course, Malcolm's mistletoe kisses.

Despite everything on her con list, she couldn't imagine waking up this morning and knowing she'd never see Malcolm again.

She turned over in bed and smiled at her pillow. What was it going to be like, to see him again? Just the two of them, in London, not Sandringham? What would they do? Would they even like each other if they were in a different context?

Would they stay in his apartment?

Of course, that was the real question in her mind. He'd mentioned it as an aside, but unless he brought it up again, how was she supposed to jump back and say, *Oh, hey, Mal-*

colm, remember when you said that thing about not wanting to presume I'd stay with you . . . ? Can you just presume?

She laughed at herself. Why had she been so comfortable being direct with him about so many other things—his feelings about the monarchy, whether he was married or not, Christmas Eve dinner—but she was strangely shy about this? She guessed it was just hard to push past how she was raised—it had been drilled into her head that nice girls didn't talk about sex, didn't want sex, didn't even like sex. As much as she'd rejected those ideas once she'd gotten older, and had tried very hard not to pass those messages along to her daughter, it was hard to fight something she'd internalized so many years ago.

She needed breakfast. She put on her leggings that felt like sweatpants, and the sweater dress that was the coziest thing she owned, and went down to the kitchen. Maddie was already there, a cup of coffee in front of her, her shoulders hunched, and her phone in her hand.

"Merry Christmas," Vivian said as she walked in.

"Happy Christmas!" Julia was standing at the stove, stirring something that smelled delicious. "Scones are on the table."

Maddie stood up and gave Vivian a hug.

"Merry Christmas, Mom." She refilled her coffee cup, went right back to her phone, and let out a sigh.

"What's so important on your phone?" Vivian asked her. "It's the middle of the night at home, isn't it?"

Maddie nodded, but didn't look away from her phone.

"I'm waiting for the pictures to come in of the royal family's walk to church. It should be any second now. The Duchess looked great when she left the house, of course, but I want to make sure the coat and the dress all worked in the wind, and the hat stayed on, and the shoes didn't make her trip, and . . . everything. I just want her to look perfect."

Maddie tightened the hand not holding her phone into a fist. Vivian sat down next to her and rubbed the back of her daughter's neck. She hadn't seen Maddie look this anxious about a client in a long time. She understood why—this was the most photographed client Maddie had ever had, and maybe *would* ever have. She crossed her fingers that the Duchess would look flawless.

Julia brought her a cup of tea, and Vivian thanked her. As much as she enjoyed the tea-making ritual, she was really going to miss having someone else make tea for her after she left Sycamore Cottage.

"Julia, I hope at some point you're going to get some time off," Vivian said. "Not that I don't love your scones, but I feel so bad sitting here with you making my breakfast on Christmas Day!"

Julia laughed.

"Don't you worry. The Duke and Duchess are going on vacation next week, and so am I. I'll be on a beach with my sister, and I promise, I won't raise a finger to do any of the cooking."

Vivian cut open a scone, and spread a layer of jam, then cream on it.

"Oh, thank God, now I don't have to feel guilty. Where—?"

"They're in!" Maddie stood up, her phone still in her hand. "They're walking. The pictures are coming in."

Julia and Vivian crowded around her to look at her phone as she scrolled through tweets from reporters and photographers.

"Oh, Maddie, she looks perfect," Vivian said. The Duchess was wearing a boat-necked navy blue dress that flared at the waist, a navy blue hat to match, with a small feather off the top, a maroon coat, loosely belted over the dress, and knee-high boots in the color Maddie had informed her more than once was called "oxblood."

"Of course she looks perfect," Maddie said. Oh good, Maddie was grinning at her phone. "I was the most worried about that hat—the feather seemed flimsy to me, and I didn't know how windy it would be today—but she insisted on it, and it seems okay. Thank God."

Maddie collapsed back into her seat, and Vivian rubbed her back.

"Good job, girl."

Maddie looked up from her phone and smiled at her.

"Thanks, Momma. And thanks for coming to spend Christmas with me here, so far away from home."

Vivian clinked her teacup against Maddie's coffee cup.

"I wouldn't have missed this for the world."

Julia took a bottle of champagne out of the fridge.

"I think it's time for mimosas, don't you two?"

Maddie drained her coffee cup and got up for more.

"Absolutely. And Julia, never tell my boyfriend I said this, but you make the best coffee I've ever had."

Julia took a big package of that ham-like English bacon out of the fridge.

"I never will, I promise. But honestly, anyone who makes coffee anywhere near as good as mine seems like a pretty good catch."

Maddie grinned.

"That he is." She looked down at her phone and laughed. "Speak of the devil, he just texted me about the Duchess's outfit."

Vivian smiled. She was so happy Maddie had found Theo.

Maddie kept scrolling through photos and—Vivian was pretty sure—texting with Theo as Julia made an enormous breakfast for the three of them. After they ate a mountain of bacon, a pile of the most perfect scrambled eggs Vivian had ever had, delicious sautéed mushrooms (which Vivian had never thought of as a breakfast food, but ate every scrap of), crispy fried potatoes, and a stack of toast to go along with all of it, Maddie stood up and yawned.

"You won't be mad if I take a nap, will you, Mom? I was up at the crack of dawn, and I'm exhausted." She pointed at Julia. "It's all your fault—I wasn't tired until just now, but after that breakfast I almost fell asleep at the table."

Vivian leaned over and gave her girl a big hug. Maddie rested her head on Vivian's shoulder, and Vivian stroked her hair the way she had when Maddie was little.

"Go take your nap. This is our relaxing Christmas, remember? And your work here in England is finally done; that means you get to rest."

Maddie sighed and smiled.

"That sounds fantastic, actually."

When Maddie stood up, Vivian sat up with a jerk.

"I just realized something! What are we going to say to the rest of the family about me staying in London? You know them, Maddie—I don't want to hear their mouths about this. I can't even tell Jo—you know she won't be able to keep it from everyone else."

Maddie grinned.

"Oh, don't worry, I already thought of that—we'll just lie to them and say we're both staying until the first. Blame it on me; tell them I told you the wrong dates. I'll just hide out at Theo's house until you get home so I don't run into anyone."

Vivian shook her head slowly.

"That's . . . brilliant, actually."

Maddie curtsied.

"I have a lot of experience in trying to keep secrets, you know."

Vivian laughed and swatted her out of the room.

Vivian tried to help Julia with the dishes, and when Julia laughed at her and shooed her out of the kitchen, she took her tea and book to her favorite chair in the sitting room.

Would she hear from Malcolm today? Would she hear from him at all before she saw him on the twenty-eighth? He'd asked for her phone number before he'd left the previous night, and she'd given it to him, but there had been people around and they kept getting interrupted, so she'd forgotten to ask him for his.

But it already felt strange to know she wouldn't see him for three days, and might not even have any contact with him at all.

She laughed at herself. Five days in a row with a man and it was like she was addicted to him. What had gotten into her? She was acting very silly, but somehow, she didn't mind at all. She smiled and opened her book.

Malcolm enjoyed his drive back to London from Sandringham a lot more than he'd enjoyed his drive there. It was Christmas Day, the sun was shining, everyone in the government was on holiday until early January and couldn't bother him, and soon he'd be spending five straight days with Vivian in London.

He smiled when he thought about the night before. With the exception of his misstep with Vivian's travel arrangements, that had been the most fun Christmas Eve he'd had in a long time. He hoped Vivian really did forgive him for doing that, and hadn't just decided to stay with him in London because her daughter had intervened. He was pretty sure from what he knew of her that she wasn't the type to just go along with something she didn't want to do, but just in case, he needed to make some excellent plans for the two of them, to ensure she had a great time. He already had a few ideas—he'd make some calls the day after Boxing Day. He smiled to himself; this was where his job came in handy.

After a quick stop at his flat to drop off his luggage and briefcase, he went straight to Sarah's. It was still early in the day, but he was looking forward to seeing everyone, and finding out what this great news was that Miles kept hinting at. He laughed as he remembered Vivian's hilarious guesses. When he parked his car, he pulled out his phone.

> Happy Christmas! Enjoying your first English
> Christmas? Looking forward to seeing you in a
> few days.

He pressed send and then he realized he hadn't given her his number the night before.

> Um, this is Malcolm, by the way.

He could almost hear her laughter in her response.

> Oh really? I never would have guessed! And
> Happy Christmas to you too! Have fun at your
> sister's. Julia is stuffing me full of food here.

He slid his phone into his pocket and rang Sarah's doorbell with a smile on his face.

She, however, was not smiling when she opened the door.

"Happy Christmas, Sarah!" he said anyway, and pulled her into a hug. She stood in his arms stiffly but dropped her head on his shoulder for a moment before she pulled away.

"Mmm. Not sure how happy it is." She shook her head and turned to walk down the hallway. "I hope you can talk some sense into him."

Oh dear. Whatever Miles's news was, Sarah was not happy about it. It was probably moving in with the girlfriend; Sarah had never liked her. He prepared himself to make peace between his sister and his nephew, once again. Luckily, he was used to that role; he'd been doing it ever since Miles was a preteen.

Malcolm followed Sarah into the kitchen and took a deep breath in. Everything smelled fantastic. He could tell the turkey was already in the oven, and there were three glorious cakes on the counter. His sister may not be a professional chef like Julia, but she was a fantastic cook. Miles sat at the table peeling potatoes.

"Help me with this, will you?" Miles said when he walked in.

"Happy Christmas to you, too," he said to his nephew.

Miles looked up at him with a grin.

"Oh right, Happy Christmas. Help peel these? I saved you a bun." Miles gestured over to the bread box.

Malcolm laughed and hunted out the bun, badly wrapped up in tinfoil next to the bread box. As he sat down at the table, Sarah deposited a cup of tea in front of him and muttered something about needing to clean the loo, then disappeared.

She was usually in the kitchen all day on holidays. She was either really upset about whatever was going on with Miles, or she'd left to give him this time to find out what was going on with Miles, and "talk some sense into him."

He grinned to himself when he thought of all of the things Sarah had wanted him to talk sense into Miles about over the years. Those trousers he'd insisted on wearing when he was thirteen, the cigarettes she'd found in his room when he was fifteen, how he wanted to do nothing but draw from ages ten to thirteen, that friend of his who was a "bad lot" when he was sixteen. For most of these things, he'd done a bit of talking sense into Miles, but he'd mostly explained to Miles how to best get along with his mother, and explained to Sarah how to deal with her son. He expected more of the same today.

He took a bite out of the bun and smiled as the icing hit his tongue. They'd had buns like this for Christmas his whole life; he was pleased Sarah still made them.

"Oh, this reminds me." He took a bag out of his pocket and tossed it to Miles. "I got you some of those sweets you like."

Miles grabbed the bag and looked up with a grin on his face.

"From that place in Norfolk? Oh wow, thank you." He laughed. "Remember that time the dog got into the bag of those sweets and ate it all when I'd only had one piece? I was so mad."

Malcolm laughed, too.

"If I remember correctly, you cried for hours about it, and refused to speak to the dog for a week."

Miles pulled a piece of candy out and popped it in his mouth.

"I was only seven!" He laughed again. "The poor dog."

"So, Miles, don't keep me in suspense." Malcolm got up from the table and got a paring knife. There was an extra peeler on the table, but he'd learned how to peel potatoes with paring knives and still thought his way was faster. "What's your big news?"

Miles dropped his peeler and beamed up at Malcolm.

"I was accepted into the London College of the Arts! My instructor this year said I had a huge amount of talent but also a huge amount to learn, so I applied, and I got a place, and with a scholarship! I start in the autumn!"

Malcolm sat down across from him.

"That is exciting, but . . . I don't understand. You'll be at Oxford next year."

Miles shook his head.

"No, no, this is instead of Oxford. I can't wait to learn more and more and devote myself to my painting. Mum keeps ragging on me, but I know that you'll—"

"Instead of Oxford?" Malcolm couldn't remember the last time he'd shouted at his nephew—probably the cigarette thing—but he couldn't help it. "Devote yourself to painting?" He shook his head and laughed. "No. You are not doing that."

Miles's lips tightened.

"Yes, I am!" He dropped the potato on the table. "I can't believe you're reacting this way. You've always been supportive of me and my art; I thought you'd be thrilled that I'm working hard and making real progress and listening to my instructor when she says—"

Malcolm sighed.

"I am supportive of you and your art, Miles. I love your paintings, I agree with your instructor when she says you have a lot of talent, and I am thrilled that you're working hard. I see nothing wrong with you planning for a future in the arts—haven't I taken you to museums hundreds of times? But you also need contingency plans. Good Lord, you're not giving up Oxford for art school. You don't get to throw your future away like this."

Miles jumped up. Thank God he was still taller than the boy, though not by much.

"It's not throwing away my future! I'm investing in my future! I know what I want my future to be, and this is how to get there—not some stuffy lecture hall or library."

Malcolm sighed.

"I know that's how you feel right now, but you have to be strategic about your career—this is your life you're talking about, not just next year. Oxford can set you up for the rest of your life; you and I both know that."

Miles threw his arms in the air. He really had gotten his flair for drama from his mother, hadn't he?

"My life? Who knows how long my life will be! My father died when he was thirty-eight; no one can say how many years I have left. I don't want to spend the rest of my life doing something I'm not passionate about—I want to enjoy every moment. I can't believe you want me to give up on my dream!"

Malcolm took a deep breath. And then another one.

"Miles. I don't want you to give up on your dream. That's

not what I'm saying. I'm saying you need to think logically about this. And while I sympathize with your feelings about your father, you need to plan for the long haul. You worked so hard to get into Oxford, and a degree there can help pave the way for so many things for the rest of your life. You can't and you won't throw that away."

Miles shoved the peeler down the table.

"I'm nineteen years old. I'm a grown man. You can't tell me what to do. Neither can my mother."

Malcolm laughed out loud.

"You're a grown man? At nineteen years old? I have some news for you—you're still a child, and you're acting like one."

"I am not!" Miles stamped to the other side of the kitchen. "You're just mad because you wanted me to go to Oxford to follow in your footsteps, then go work in some stuffy office somewhere and shuffle papers all day, just like you do. I don't want to be like you. I want to live my life! You've never had any dreams; you don't know what it's like to have them, unless your dream was to be at the beck and call of that old woman!" He stopped by the door. "I thought you were better than this. I trusted you! But you're just like all the rest."

He stormed out of the kitchen, and a few seconds later, Malcolm heard the front door slam. He dropped his head in his hands.

Chapter Nine

Malcolm walked into the lobby of The Goring hotel at 11:55 a.m. on December 28. He'd realized the day before that he and Vivian hadn't communicated since those quick texts early on Christmas Day, so he'd texted her and arranged to meet her at her hotel at noon. He'd been so consumed with everything going on with Miles that he hadn't thought of it until then.

Miles hadn't come back home on Christmas Day until after Malcolm had left. Malcolm was pretty sure Miles had spent the day at his girlfriend's house, but he had no idea. And to top it all off, Sarah had also been furious at him—she'd apparently been counting on him to make the situation with Miles better, not worse. He'd spent days getting angry texts from her, all of which just served to make him more frustrated and upset about this whole situation.

Malcolm knew he should have handled the conversation with Miles differently. He didn't think he'd ever yelled like that at Miles in his life. But he'd been so shocked and blindsided, he hadn't been able to think straight.

He sighed. He'd spent his whole career—maybe his whole life—successfully avoiding conflict. He'd even managed to have a conflict-free divorce, for God's sake! And he'd somehow blown that all up in one conversation.

He just hoped he could put this whole thing out of his head for the next few days and enjoy this time with Vivian.

Speaking of Vivian, here was another situation where he didn't know exactly what was going on, or how to resolve it. He'd hoped she'd be spending these few days with him, at his flat, but she'd never really addressed that part of his invitation. So he supposed he'd just see if she brought her luggage down today when she met him in the lobby.

Where was she? He glanced at his watch. 12:02. He had said noon in his text, hadn't he? He pulled out his phone and scrolled down to their texts. Yes, definitely, he had. Should he text her? Or call up to her room?

12:05. Something must be wrong.

Had she changed her mind? Maybe she'd left with Maddie this morning and hadn't told him.

No, Vivian wouldn't do that.

At least, he didn't think she would.

He had gotten the hotel correct, hadn't he? He found the

email that the Duchess's private secretary had sent him with the Forests' travel information. Yes, The Goring. Well, maybe . . .

"Malcolm! Sorry I'm late. I hope you haven't been waiting long!"

There she was, walking to him from the elevator, with a smile on her face.

He smiled at her, so relieved she was here and not on her way back to California that he was almost not annoyed at her casual lateness. And almost not disappointed she had no luggage by her side.

"Not a problem. Are you ready?"

She smiled at him.

"That depends on what we're doing today." She cocked her head at him. "What *are* we doing today?"

His original plan had been that they'd swing by his flat to drop off her luggage before they did anything else, but that didn't seem to be necessary. He'd have to quickly revise his plan.

He opened the hotel door for her.

"How do you feel about surprises?"

She laughed.

"I hate surprises."

He stopped on the sidewalk and turned to her.

"Are you . . . do you really?"

She nodded.

"For the most part, absolutely." She shrugged. "Well, you asked! So often, surprises are just a way for someone to do something they're not sure you would like, so they present it to you as a fait accompli so you can't argue with them about it. And even worse, you have to put on a happy face, because 'It's a surprise!' so you're supposed to be thrilled about it, and you look like a jerk when you're not. There have been a handful of times in my life when a surprise was thoughtful, someone thinking about what would make me happy. But too often, it's them thinking about themselves. The problem is so often surprises are about the other person and what they want, and not the person they're surprising."

Oh. Splendid. Just splendid.

She patted him on the shoulder.

"Oh God, you look crestfallen. I'm not saying all surprises are bad! I have had a few good ones . . ."

He knew when women said things just to humor him. Now he had no fucking idea what he was going to do. And now the one bright spot in his week had been ruined. Fantastic.

The surprises he'd planned for Vivian had been the only things he'd been happy about all week. He'd made a bunch of calls and pulled a bunch of strings to get things perfect, and now he didn't know what to do.

Vivian caught herself before she let out a sigh. She probably shouldn't have been honest with Malcolm about that, but it wasn't in her nature anymore to lie about her feelings. Though now she was worried that she'd ruined everything.

She had no real idea about how the next few days would

go. She and Malcolm had texted a little bit on Christmas Day, but then not again until yesterday. She'd even worried that the plan to have her stay on in London was off, until she'd gotten that rather curt text from him that he'd meet her in the lobby of her hotel at noon. She'd wanted to ask if she was invited to stay with him, but it felt strange to ask that over a text, and his demeanor this afternoon had been pretty chilly so far. She'd packed her suitcase before coming downstairs this morning but had lost her nerve and had left it, all packed, in her hotel room.

She couldn't fight back the sigh this time. She'd thought she was going to have sex tonight! She'd looked forward to it! But Malcolm had barely touched her so far, so that seemed less and less likely by the moment.

"Where did you and Maddie go in your two days in London?" Malcolm asked after they'd gotten in the car.

Oh, thank God, something to talk about.

"Want to see?" She pulled out her phone and narrated some of the pictures she and Maddie had taken over the past few days: their walk along the Thames; their trip to Liberty department store; their dinner out; their visit to the British Museum; their selfie outside of Buckingham Palace; their fancy tea.

"We went to this really fun place for tea, so colorful and creative—see? Look how cute it is. But the food was great, too: there were cucumber sandwiches and smoked salmon sandwiches and these incredible curry chicken sandwiches, and oh, the egg salad sandwiches were the best I've ever had.

The pastries were so pretty it was almost a shame to eat them, but the scones weren't as good as Julia's."

They'd really fit a lot into their two days in London— they'd treated themselves to blowouts, which gave them lots of time for a good hairdresser's chair gossip; they'd done a lot of shopping, for themselves and for presents for the family; and they'd just had time to relax together. She and Maddie hadn't had this much one-on-one time in years. Maybe once she had a handle on the new job, and felt like she could take an actual vacation, they could go somewhere again, just the two of them.

But who knew what Maddie's life would be like then? Would she have the time for another vacation with her mom? Would her job be too busy for that? Given all the attention she'd gotten from her work with the Duchess, that was a possibility. Or would she be married? Or have kids? The way everything with Theo was going, that could all easily happen. Vivian would love it if any or all of those things came true for Maddie. But the thought that this may have been their last solo trip together made tears spring to her eyes.

She forced herself to shake that melancholy off and concentrate on telling Malcolm the story of their whirlwind trip. But after a few minutes, she realized Malcolm had hardly responded at all. Was he just being polite when he'd asked her what they'd done? She moved away from him and dropped her phone back into her purse.

"Sorry. You probably didn't want to know in that much detail. Or with that many visuals."

He leaned away from her, too.

"No, that was fine. You and your daughter take a lot of pictures together."

Was that a criticism? Was he making fun of her penchant for taking selfies with Maddie? She didn't used to do that, but since Maddie was so into the Instagram thing, she always made Vivian take selfies with her whenever they went somewhere together. At first, Vivian had been really self-conscious about it. But then Maddie had taught her how to look good in a selfie—Chin up! Picture from above! Smile with your eyes!—and she'd gotten into it. Now she found it fun to have a record of all of the places she and Maddie had gone together, whether it was London or a beach day or just a happy hour on a random night when they were both free. She was suddenly annoyed with Malcolm for criticizing her relationship with her daughter.

"We do take a lot of pictures together," she said. "We like them."

Why did things feel so awkward between her and Malcolm today? Was it that she hadn't seen him in days, and she'd forgotten what she'd liked about him? Or was this a disaster in the making? She needed to do what she always advised other people to do and take a few deep breaths and reframe her attitude.

"How was your Christmas?" she asked him. "Did you have a good time at your sister's?" She suddenly remembered something. "Oh, what was your nephew's big news?"

He shrugged and took a minute to answer.

"Oh, just some good news about his painting. He's more excited about it than anyone else, which is often the case for teenagers, I've learned."

Okay, that conversational gambit hadn't succeeded in her goal to improve their vibe today. Fine, she'd let him take the lead.

The day didn't get much better. They drove down to the river and took a boat ride down the Thames—she took a lot of pictures, but after what Malcolm had said about her pictures with Maddie, she felt too shy to take any of him. Plus, it was freezing cold on that boat. Afterward, they stopped for tea, and they were a little more relaxed with each other, but when she made a reference to Julia's scones on Christmas Day, he froze up again.

From there, they went to Westminster Abbey, which she was excited to see; she was even more excited when the priest at the door smiled at Malcolm and waved them in past the long line of people waiting to get inside. But the whole time they walked through the huge, historic, gorgeous church, he barely spoke to her. For a while, she commented to him about the architecture, and the beauty of the church, and the facts she learned on the tour, but his responses were so brief it made her feel like he didn't want to be there. At one point, they sat together silently and stared up at the altar. She looked at his unsmiling profile and tried to figure out what was wrong. Was he bored of playing tour guide? Or did he regret asking her to stay? Was that what this was about?

She sighed as they walked out of the Abbey. This wasn't

why she was in thirty-two-degree London and not on her way to sixty-two-degree California. What happened to all of their fun banter and laughter? Why did Malcolm seem like he was on a forced march of sightseeing instead of a relaxed romantic visit, which is what she *thought* this was? And for the love of God, why hadn't he seemed to even think about kissing her all day?

She never should have stayed. Why had she listened to her daughter?

Malcolm had completely forgotten he'd told Vivian that Miles had big news to share. When she'd brought it up, he'd said the first thing he could think of and changed the subject. He didn't want to ruin their day and tell her the whole long Miles story. He didn't want to get into their fight, or his subsequent fight with Sarah, and how angry and hurt he'd been about Miles's parting shots at him. He just wanted to relax and have fun with Vivian and not think about his pain-in-the-ass nephew.

Unfortunately, that was impossible. Every time he tried to relax, he thought of something he should have said to Miles, or a way he could have handled the whole situation better, or felt a wave of fury at Miles for throwing his life away like this, or got angry again with Sarah for not telling him in advance what Miles's big news was, so he'd be prepared for it. Or, when he managed to forget about his family and turn his attention to the bright, lovely woman sitting across from him, she brought up Christmas Day, and it made all of his anger—at Miles, at Sarah, at himself—resurface.

He wanted to apologize to Vivian for how preoccupied he was, but he didn't want to get into a whole conversation about why. What was he supposed to say? *Sorry, Vivian, I blew up at my nephew and laughed at him and his ambitions and he's furious at me now, and it's all my fault that he's going to ruin his life just to spite me.*

No, he definitely couldn't say that. And he didn't want to lie to her. Better to say nothing at all.

Plus, he was upset she'd decided not to stay with him. And he supposed he'd have to tell her about the surprise he had in store for her.

The next few days were not going to be what he'd hoped for.

Finally, they made it to their dinner reservation. He was pleased he'd gotten a reservation here for him and Vivian; the food was fantastic, the service was lovely, and it was the kind of London restaurant he wanted her to experience—an upscale Nigerian restaurant that was definitely not the type of place most Americans thought of when they thought of London. He really hoped she'd like it.

The man who barged into the restaurant behind them, however, was going to make that very difficult. Just as Malcolm greeted the host, who he'd met many times, the newcomer pushed past Malcolm like he wasn't even there. He slammed his hand on the host's table.

"Wilston-Jeffries, party of two. My secretary called earlier."

The host looked at Malcolm, then back at the guy. Malcolm knew his type all too well. The worst thing about his type was they almost always got their way.

"I'll be with you in a moment, sir."

Malcolm liked a lot about his job. The diplomacy, being involved in national politics and foreign affairs, the history, the people he worked with (well, some of them). But the number one best thing about his job was when guys like this one thought they could push past him and treat him like nothing, but everyone else around him knew he worked for the Queen. Like he'd said to Vivian when they were at Sandringham, he had complicated feelings about the monarchy, but it was excellent for him in situations like this one.

The host turned back to Malcolm.

"Please, follow me, sir."

Wilston-Jeffries beckoned his date.

"Come on. This way. I think our table is over there."

The host stopped him.

"Just a moment, sir. Your table is not yet ready. Wait here." He turned away without another word. "Mr. Hudson? Please, come with me."

They were seated at a table in the corner of the restaurant, and their waiter immediately brought over glasses of champagne.

"I believe you enjoy this vintage, sir," the waiter said.

Vivian wiggled her eyebrows at him and picked up her glass.

He hadn't brought Vivian here to impress her with his

consequence. She'd been at Sandringham for days; if she was impressed by anyone's consequence, it certainly wasn't going to be his.

But . . . it had been really nice to be kowtowed to with her by his side, he had to admit.

Unfortunately, the asshole from earlier was seated at the table next to theirs. The waiter glanced at Malcolm and silently shook his head in apology.

"Where's the injera? I don't see it on the menu. Does it just come with all of the dishes?" Wilston-Jeffries asked the waiter.

The waiter took an almost imperceptible moment to answer.

"We don't serve injera, sir. That's an Ethiopian bread; it doesn't come from our tradition."

The man huffed at his date.

"I was looking forward to introducing you to injera and teaching you how to eat with it!" He turned back to the waiter. "Well, what's your spiciest dish? I want it really spicy, you know, like the kind you'd have."

Malcolm looked at Vivian, who was staring straight back at him. Her eyes were huge, and he could tell she was fighting back laughter. Maybe this guy wasn't going to ruin their dinner after all.

The waiter pointed at a line on the menu.

"It's this soup, sir. However, we advise—"

"No need for advice. I know it all. And add some of your hottest peppers to it!"

The waiter nodded.

"And you, ma'am?"

His date requested something much less spicy, and Malcolm saw the man puff out his chest like a bird. Vivian's cough seemed like much more of a chuckle, so he could tell she saw it, too.

They'd both spent so much time focused on the table next to them and not their menus, that when the waiter came over to their table, neither of them had decided what to order.

"Shall we start with some wine while we decide?" he asked Vivian, who nodded.

Malcolm picked a bottle of wine at random to give them more time.

Vivian leaned forward and lowered her voice.

"Okay, I love spicy food, but now I absolutely can't ask what's spicy and what isn't. I don't want to be that guy."

Malcolm now had to cough/laugh himself.

"Don't worry, I've been here before. I can tell you. The menu has changed since the last time I was here, but I honestly think you'll like everything, and if you've never had Nigerian food before"—he looked at her questioningly, and she shook her head—"I think this will be a fun new experience."

She smiled at him. This was one of the most genuine smiles she'd given him all day. He was suddenly grateful for the pompous ass next to them for breaking the tension between the two of them.

"I'm happy to try anything. All that walking around today made me starving. I can't wait."

He smiled back at her as the waiter returned with their wine.

She lifted her glass and clinked it with his, and his shoulders lost some of their tension. Maybe the next few days would be good after all.

"Sir, ma'am, are you ready to order?"

Malcolm raised his eyebrow at Vivian, and she smiled up at the waiter. They ordered everything that looked good to both of them, and he was suddenly starving. He'd barely eaten at lunch, because of how preoccupied he'd been, and Vivian was right; they had walked around a lot today.

"I just can't help it—I have an extraordinary palate and a very high spice tolerance. Many people have commented on it."

Wow, the guy next to them was still on about this. Vivian stared straight at Malcolm, her lips sealed together and her eyes dancing. Malcolm did all he could not to smile back at her.

"Um . . ." He had to think of something for them to talk about, so they wouldn't spend all of dinner laughing at this man. "What was your favorite thing we saw today?"

She winked at him and smiled.

"I really loved Westminster Abbey," she said. "Partly because it was beautiful, and there was so much history there, but also because despite all of that, and all of the tourists, it still felt like a church, if you know what I mean?"

He poured more wine into her glass.

"I do," he said. "I've been to famous old churches when there are too many people there, and it feels like just any kind of building—like it's divorced from its original purpose. But Westminster Abbey still feels like a church to me, too, despite the long lines and many tourists walking around. It's one of my favorite places in London." He looked down into his glass of wine. "Sometimes, when I used to work in Parliament and was having a hard day, I would walk over there, go inside, and just . . . sit in one of the pews for a while. I don't know if I was praying, or meditating, or whatever you would call it, but it felt like having the centuries-old stones around me would help. I don't know if they gave me perspective, or just absorbed my stress, but whatever it was, it made a difference." He shrugged. Now he felt silly for confessing this to her. "That probably sounds . . ."

"Smart? Relatable? Like something more of us should do?" She nodded. "Yes, it sounds like all of those things."

He reached across the table and touched her hand, just for a second.

"Thanks. I should probably find a way to do something like that more often."

She nodded.

"Me too. I used to go to church pretty regularly, but I got busy and out of the habit. I miss it. It gave me that time of peace that you're talking about. Life can get so"—she sighed—"overwhelming sometimes, with everything going on in the world, then dealing with difficult issues at work, and then always family. It helps to take time for yourself, though I don't take my own advice on that as often as I should. I do go on long walks, which is a good break for me in that way."

He laughed.

"I could tell. I could barely keep up with you this afternoon! And I know you usually go on walks in much more moderate temperatures than London in December."

She looked down, then back up at him. He loved how, despite her directness, she occasionally got shy with him.

"I was just in Norfolk in December, don't you remember? London weather is balmy compared to that."

The appetizers arrived at the table next to them. They both looked sideways at the table.

"Please let us know if your starter is to your liking, sir," the waiter said.

"Oh, I'll make it very clear, don't you worry about that," their neighbor said.

He took a spoonful of his soup.

"Hmm. It's all right, but I thought I made it clear that I wanted something very spicy," he said to the hovering waiter.

The waiter nodded.

"You did, sir, you did. I would give it a few more spoonfuls before you judge."

The man huffed and ate a few more spoonfuls in quick succession.

"Ah." He nodded. His bald head shimmered under the restaurant lights. "That's better. Very spicy, just as I like it."

The waiter bowed.

"Very good, sir."

The waiter came around to their table and filled up their water glasses. Malcolm kept glancing over at their neighbor, and he noticed Vivian did, too. He ate a few more bites of the soup, but his face got pinker and pinker. After a few minutes, he put his spoon down.

"Well," he said to his date, "finally, a place where they listen to me about how I like my food to be served." He picked up his full water glass and downed it. "I'm sure most people couldn't handle even a bite of this soup." Sweat formed on his forehead and dripped down his face. His head got even shinier. He picked up his date's water glass without asking her and drank all of that, too. "Waiter! More water over here!"

Vivian looked at Malcolm, her eyes wide. Malcolm could tell they both knew exactly what was going on.

The waiter came over, with such a bland look on his face that Malcolm knew—if he'd had any doubt before—that the staff was just as irritated by this guy as he was.

"Certainly, sir. Is your soup to your liking?"

Their neighbor grabbed the water glass almost before the waiter had finished pouring.

"Mmmhmm," he said as he drank both glassfuls on the table again.

Malcolm grinned at Vivian and poured them more wine.

Vivian was going to explode from all of her held-in laughter. This man next to them was clearly about to faint because of how spicy the food was, but he wouldn't confess it for the life of him. If he hadn't been so terrible before, she would have leaned over and told him that drinking water just made spicy food hotter, and instead he should eat some rice or bread or dairy to soothe himself. But instead, she just drank more wine and watched the show.

"You'll have to tell me how you like the food," Malcolm said, when their starters arrived. "I hope it's not too spicy for you."

She took a bite, then grinned at him.

"It is very spicy, but it's perfect, thank you. Just enough to wake up my taste buds and make me a little giddy, but not enough to bring tears to my eyes."

Malcolm looked away from her and coughed again. Their neighbor currently had tears streaming from his eyes, which he was attempting to disguise with his napkin. Even his date couldn't stop staring at him. The best part was that his bravado wouldn't allow him to stop eating the soup completely, so every so often he would take a deep breath and eat another spoonful, and his face just got redder and redder.

"Cameron, are you feeling all right?" his date finally asked him.

"Fine. Fine, couldn't be better," he said, his shirt wet with sweat.

She sat back and nodded and didn't say anything else for a second.

"Well, I only asked because I'm not feeling that well. Would it trouble you too much if you took me home now? It's possible something here didn't agree with me."

Ohhh, that was good. This woman knew how to deal with difficult men. Vivian shook her head. That was probably not a great thing for her; it most likely meant that poor woman had dealt with far too many difficult men in the course of her life, and she knew how to get them out of a situation they'd caused without injury to their ego. But still, she'd done it very well.

"Oh, of course I can take you home now! It's this restaurant, I'm sure—I knew there was something wrong with this place as soon as we stepped foot inside. Waiter!"

The waiter was at his side within seconds.

"Yes, sir?"

"We have to leave immediately. Something was wrong with my guest's meal, and she isn't feeling well." He threw his credit card down on the table. "Please bring us the bill this moment."

The waiter bowed.

"Certainly, sir. And of course, there's no charge for your food, only for the drinks."

The man gulped another glass of water and waved him away.

Moments later, the waiter brought over the bill, and the man signed his name and raced to the door, without bothering to wait for his date. She followed him slowly, and stopped to thank the waiter on her way out. Vivian hoped this poor woman cut this guy loose after tonight.

As soon as the door closed behind them, Vivian and Malcolm looked at each other and burst into laughter. Vivian was just winding down when she looked over at Malcolm and saw the tears streaming down his face, and that started her up all over again.

"I'm sorry," he choked out. "I just can't stop thinking about how he kept drinking all that water."

She wiped away her own tears.

"I can't stop thinking about how much pain he'll be in later tonight."

Malcolm practically howled at that, which just made Vivian laugh harder.

Their laughter finally subsided when the waiter came over and set a dish in the middle of their table.

"Compliments of the chef, and his apologies for"—the waiter cleared his throat—"any unpleasantness earlier. I hope you're both enjoying your meal?"

Vivian beamed at the waiter.

"It's wonderful, thank you so much. I've never had Nigerian food before, and everything we've had so far is delicious. Please thank the chef for me." She paused. "And it's the ideal amount of spice for me."

He grinned at her.

"Happy to hear that." He nodded at Malcolm and disappeared.

Any awkwardness that had lingered from the afternoon was now long gone. For the rest of the dinner, he told her stories about when he'd worked in Parliament, she told him stories about her funniest cases, and their accidental touches of each other's hands and knees got more and more frequent.

They shared not two, but three desserts, and each had a glass of port to go along with it. When Vivian walked out into the cold London night, she was in love with Nigerian food, London, and all forms of fermented grapes. She put the hood of her coat up against the gentle rain, slid her arm into Malcolm's, and smiled at the world.

"What a great restaurant," she said. "No wonder you like it."

He pulled her closer to him.

"Nothing like that has ever happened to me there! All I knew was that the food was delicious and the service was charming. I didn't realize we'd get a show tonight, too."

Vivian chuckled as they walked toward his car.

"I thought I was going to die if I had to hold my laughter in for one more second, Malcolm! When he kept eating the soup! Every time he picked up the spoon with this deep breath, like he was summoning up all of his energy. I'm surprised he didn't catch me laughing at him."

Malcolm chuckled as he opened his car door for her.

"Men like that never think anyone could be laughing at them. That's why it's so fun to do it."

On the way back to the hotel, Malcolm took a detour so they'd see some of London all lit up at night. She loved driving through cities at night, especially when she wasn't the one driving, and could just look around and see the buildings aglow, and the bridges outlined by the stars, and the blackness of the river gleaming in the moonlight.

When they got back to the hotel, Vivian didn't want the night to end.

"Do you want to come upstairs for a nightcap?" she said, before she could reconsider. She immediately wished she had reconsidered. A nightcap??? Who the hell did she think she was, some sort of star in a comedy from the 1940s? She'd never used that word before in her life!

But Malcolm immediately nodded.

"That's a lovely idea," he said. "Should we get the bar to make some hot toddies for us?"

Vivian nodded.

"Yes, absolutely. It's chilly out there."

Malcolm beckoned over the bartender as they walked by the bar, and moments later he held two of the fanciest hot toddies she'd ever seen.

They walked to the elevators, arm in arm. When they got inside the elevator, she smiled at him.

"I didn't know hotel bars would make drinks for you to bring upstairs; I was only thinking of the minibar. See how much I learn from you?"

He laughed.

"Oh, most hotel bars will do that, but one thing I've learned in my job is that you can get anyone to do just about anything if a) you give them enough money, or b) they think you're important." He winked at her. "And they do know me here."

She held up her finger.

"That makes me think of something else I've been meaning to bring up: Maddie was certain she'd booked us just a regular room with two beds, but somehow we were booked in a suite. Do you know anything about that?"

He shrugged, but the smile never left his eyes.

"I imagine they realized when you checked in that you were American—London hotel rooms are often too small for Americans. I'm sure they just wanted to accommodate you."

She rolled her eyes as the elevator doors opened.

"Mmm. I'm sure that's it."

She pulled out her room key and unlocked the door of the suite.

"See? We have this little sitting room here, with a couch and everything, in addition to our pretty sizable bedroom. Do you—"

Oh no. Oh no, why hadn't she remembered before she brought him up to her room that she'd packed everything this morning and had left her suitcase right in the middle of the sitting room?

Maybe he'd think it was empty, and she'd just moved it there when Maddie was packing up to go. Maybe he wouldn't realize she'd packed everything in anticipation/hope of going to his apartment.

"Vivian? What's your suitcase doing there?" He poked his head into the open door of the bedroom. "Are you all packed? Were you planning to leave tomorrow?"

His face was wooden again, just like it had been this morning. The only thing she could do here was come clean with the truth.

"No. I mean, yes, maybe, but not . . ." She sighed. "When you first brought up the idea of me staying in London, you made a reference to staying with you, and I didn't know if . . . I hoped that . . . but it's okay, I understand if that's not what you really want—"

Before she finished her sentence, Malcolm was kissing her so hard she could barely breathe.

Vivian wrapped her arms around him and kissed him back just as hard. Breathing was overrated.

When he finally came up for air, they looked at each other, and both started laughing.

Malcolm brushed her hair back from her face.

"Vivian. Would you like to stay with me for the rest of your time in London?"

She shook her head. The smile dropped from Malcolm's face, and he took a step back.

"Oh. Sorry, I thought—"

She held a finger in front of his lips.

"You didn't let me talk. I'd love to stay with you, starting tomorrow. But tonight there's no way either one of us is leaving this hotel room."

She pushed him down onto the couch.

Chapter Ten

It took surprisingly little time for Malcolm to get Vivian's clothes off. Not that Malcolm had thought he would be slow about that, but given that they barely took their hands and lips off of each other, he was impressed with himself.

Vivian was pretty industrious herself; he barely noticed her fingers on his shirt, but before he even sat up, she'd pushed it to the floor.

But he absolutely noticed her fingers at his waist. She undid his belt and pulled down his zipper. Before she could get any further, he stood up, threw the rest of his clothes off, and pulled her back on top of him.

They stayed on the couch for a long time, kissing, touching, exploring each other's bodies. He loved seeing what made her gasp, what made her sigh, what made her giggle. And he really loved feeling her, at first tentative, then more confident, hands and lips on him. She ran her hands up and down his hips, then over the length of his hard cock, slowly, then faster and faster. He shook his head and stood up.

"Why are we on this cramped little couch when there's a great big bed in the other room?" He reached out a hand to her, and she took it.

"Excellent question, Mr. Hudson." She looked up and down the length of his body and smiled. "All of that horseback riding seems to be treating you well."

He grinned, and looked straight at her.

"Whatever you are doing looks tremendous on you, Ms. Forest."

She shook her head.

"Thank you for saying that, but . . ."

He took her hand and moved it down the length of his body again.

"Does that feel like I'm 'saying that'? I didn't spend the past week spending every possible second thinking about this moment to just be 'saying that,' do you understand?"

She lifted her face to his and kissed him on the lips.

"You were right. It's definitely time to move to the bed."

Vivian pulled back the covers and then stopped.

"No. Oh no." She turned to him. "Do you have condoms?"

Shit. Shit shit shit shit shit.

"No. I didn't realize today would end like this!"

She laughed.

"Well, part of me is grateful you didn't presume, but the part of me that wants to have sex right now is furious you weren't more prepared." She looked around the room. "I always tell women they should be prepared themselves, and here I am not taking my own advice. But in my defense, I didn't think to pack condoms on a trip to England with my daughter!"

He was also furious with himself for not being more prepared.

"Well, there are things we can do that don't necessitate a condom," he said.

She laughed.

"Oh, the enthusiasm!"

He squeezed her ass, and she giggled again.

"I am very enthusiastic about all of the things we could do tonight, with or without a condom; I just wish we could do them all!" He kissed her hair. "Or we could put our clothes back on and go back to my apartment?"

She pushed him away and held up a finger.

"I have a better idea."

She walked over to the minibar and picked up a box.

"I saw this the day we checked in and completely forgot about it until right now. It's a 'personal care' box, and"—she tore open the box and looked up at him with a grin—"there are two condoms inside! God bless us, every one."

He grabbed her and kissed her hard.

"You, Ms. Vivian Forest, are brilliant and observant, as

well as being charming and altogether too sexy for your own good." He fell with her onto the bed and rolled over on top of her.

"If you just said that to ensure we make good use of these, well . . . okay, fine, I'm in." She smiled from underneath him and slid her hands down his body until she reached his butt, then squeezed.

He laughed out loud.

"I would have said that no matter what, but your reaction to it shows me exactly why I've been smitten with you since the first moment I saw you." He crawled down her body and kissed her neck, her collarbone, then lingered for a very long time at her breasts, until her moans got so loud he had to keep moving down.

She let out that giggle again when he got there, but her laughter quickly turned into sighs and then moans again, and her hands clutched his head until she gasped and her whole body relaxed.

He slid back to the head of the bed, and she put her arms around him and laughed.

"What's so funny?" he asked as he pulled her toward him.

He could feel her smile against his chest.

"Everything about this is funny in the best possible way," she said. "That we met each other in the first place, that you took me horseback riding, that you managed to convince me to stay in England, that the man who introduced me to the Queen gave me the best orgasm I've had in years." She laughed again. "This whole situation is hilarious and I love it."

She sat up, reached over to the side of the bed, and grabbed one of the condoms from the hotel kit.

"And while I very much appreciate you giving me a moment to rest just there, I don't want to let these condoms go to waste. Do you?"

Oh, he liked this woman so much. He sat up and took the condom from her hand.

"Absolutely not."

He tore the package open. Not his favorite brand, but he would take anything at this point. She watched him roll the condom on, and if it was possible for him to get harder, her steady gaze on his cock would have accomplished it.

She pulled him toward her and kissed him. As they kissed, he pushed her slowly back onto the bed, so he was on top of her again. She had that wicked smile on her face once more as he pushed inside of her, then she closed her eyes and her smile softened.

"Mmm. That feels so good."

She'd taken the words right out of his mouth.

They moved together, first slowly, as they both figured each other out. Did she like it like this . . . or like that? Did she like it when he touched her here, too, or was that too much? He could tell she was making the same calculations about him, which made him like her even more.

But soon, it felt too good for him to keep thinking. He just moved, harder and harder, and the way she moved with him and clutched at him and whispered into his ear told him how much she liked all of this.

Finally, he thrust everything he had into her and let out a loud yell into the pillow. He collapsed back onto the bed and pulled her on top of him.

"Wow," he said, when he could breathe again.

She kissed his shoulder.

"My thoughts exactly."

The next morning, Vivian woke up with the blankets tucked around her and Malcolm breathing softly next to her. She looked at him, still sound asleep, sighed in contentment, then grinned up at the ceiling.

Who would have ever thought that she, Vivian Forest, would wake up on December 29 in a fancy hotel room in London, in bed with a very attractive man? She certainly wouldn't have thought so. But here she was, and goodness, was she happy about it.

Thank God Maddie had made her stay in London. What if she'd been scared and stubborn and had flown home with Maddie the day before and had missed out on last night? She shuddered to think about it.

She got up and went to the bathroom, then slid back under the covers next to Malcolm. He opened his eyes and pulled her close to him.

"Good morning." He kissed her shoulder, her cheek, her forehead.

"Good morning." She smiled up at him. "I believe we have one more condom. What do you say to—"

Before she could finish her sentence, he growled and pulled her underneath him, as she giggled again. How was this man able to both make her laugh this much and turn her on this much?

After a very successful use of the last condom, they curled back up in bed together. Malcolm kissed her on the cheek.

"So. We have three more full days together, and I think we would both agree that most of yesterday didn't go so well." He sat up, turned to her, and took a deep breath. "And that's all my fault."

She sat up, too.

"No, Malcolm, it wasn't—"

He stopped her.

"Please don't argue with me; we both know it's true. But let me explain why." He sighed. "I lied to you yesterday."

She just waited. Whatever this was, it was a big deal to him.

"About Miles. That's not what his big news was. It was that he'd gotten into an art school for next year and is giving up his place at Oxford." Her mouth dropped open, and he nodded. "Yes, that's exactly how I felt. We had a massive fight about it. And now he's even more determined to do this, Sarah is furious at me for encouraging him with his art in the first place, and for not finding a way to talk him out of this, and I'm furious at both Miles and myself."

It was obviously very hard for him to tell her this. She was grateful he trusted her enough to open up to her. She reached for his hand, and he squeezed it.

"This all sounds so hard. Do you want to tell me how it happened?"

He turned on his elbow toward her and nodded.

"Rather strangely, I do." And then the whole story spilled out of him—about how excited his nephew had been, how perplexed and then angry Malcolm had been, what Miles had said about passion and his father, what Malcolm had said about securing his future, how they'd both yelled, how Miles had stormed out.

"I'm sorry, Malcolm." She took his hand.

He kissed hers, then smiled at her.

"Thanks. I'm sorry for taking all of this out on you yesterday. I've been in a foul mood since Christmas Day, trying to figure out what to do and how to fix it and if Miles is ruining his life, and if I've ruined our relationship forever. I thought spending time with you would help push it all out of my head, but instead your questions about Miles and your happy stories about your daughter just made me think about everything I did wrong. And plus . . ."

He opened his mouth to say something more, but instead just shook his head.

"Plus what? Really, you can tell me," she said.

He let out a huge sigh.

"This is also why your thing about surprises caught me off guard yesterday, and I'm sorry I acted like such a boor about it. But the only thing I've done in the past few days, other than fret about the situation with Miles, was to plan a few small things for us, and I was looking forward to surprising you, so when you said that, I didn't know what to do." He laughed. "Which of course means everything you said about surprises is completely right—my desire to surprise you *is* all about me, and not you. Ouch. Right, here were my plans—"

This time, she stopped him.

"Wait. I said all of that off the cuff. I hadn't realized you had actually planned surprises for me. Why don't I tell you exactly what I hate about surprises, and we can see if we can figure out a way to make this work for both of us."

He ran his fingers through her very tangled ponytail.

"You're so good at problem-solving. I feel like Parliament could use you." He shook his head. "No, they'd never listen to someone as logical as you. All right, tell me everything you hate."

More people should ask her to do that.

"Okay, for starters, there's so much managing someone else's emotions along with your own. You have to monitor your facial expression so well, and make sure it's reflecting what it's supposed to reflect, and as you may have noticed about me, I have a pretty expressive face." He laughed, and she grinned at him. "You've noticed, have you? Here's an example of that: I was so relieved that my boss emailed me that he was going to retire and he wanted me to become director after him. I was so taken aback by the email, I almost dropped my tea. If he'd told me in person, and I didn't manage to get ahold of myself quickly enough, he might have thought I was horrified by the idea of the job."

Malcolm nodded.

"That makes sense. What else?"

"I hate that everything is out of my hands." She ticked off her fingers. "Where I'm going, what I'm doing, even often who I'm with. There's nothing I hate more than a surprise party, where you're never in the clothes you would want to be wearing, someone always invited a person you hate, and you have to do the whole gasp, huge smile, 'Oh my God!' thing."

She glanced at him and sighed.

"I can see what you're thinking, and yes indeed, my ex did throw me surprise parties on more than one occasion, and yes, I hated them every single time, and yes, we did get in fights after every single one, because I didn't appreciate everything he did to throw the parties. But those parties were about him, not me. It took me a long time to realize that."

He kept running his fingers through her hair.

"Was this Maddie's dad?"

She nodded.

"Yeah, Maddie's dad. He and I broke up when Maddie was little, but we'd been together for a while before that. Granted, we broke up thirty years ago, but I guess there are some things that stick around."

It felt ridiculous, but she'd never connected the dots before about her hatred of surprises and the way her ex always reacted when he threw her those surprise parties. She always had to apologize to him when she didn't enjoy them, when he knew she hated them.

She looked back over at Malcolm to see how he was taking all of this decades-old baggage she'd just dumped on him.

He didn't seem fazed at all.

"Well, I can promise a few things: There will be absolutely no surprise parties. I will tell you what to wear—within reason, to be clear! You can wear what you want, but I can give you . . . guidelines, how about that? And you are under no obligation to appreciate or thank me for any of this—remember, if we do it, it's because you're doing *me* a favor, not because I'm doing one for you."

She laughed at that, but he looked serious.

"No, really, I mean it. Please feel free to tell me that actually, no, you want to approve everything, and I'll be happy to tell you. But if you don't, I know that it's because you've taken pity on me and my dreadful week, and I appreciate it."

She kissed his cheek.

"That's not the only reason. It's also because I trust you. You can have your surprises, but I'd better get those outfit guidelines!"

He laughed.

"Okay, I promise. Now"—he looked at his watch—"I scheduled a private tour of Buckingham Palace for us at ten thirty today. I'm happy to call to cancel if you—"

"Seriously? A private tour of Buckingham Palace?" Maddie was going to DIE when she told her. "They said they weren't doing any tours right now!"

He grinned.

"I may or may not have some pull in that area. Is that a yes? Do you want to go?"

She jumped out of bed.

"What time is it? Are we running late? I take really fast showers."

The smile on his face was so wide and warm she felt it down to her toes.

"It's only nine, so we have plenty of time. We can toss your suitcase in the boot of my car and bring it to my flat afterward."

She smiled back at him.

"Perfect."

A little over an hour later, they drove down the wide street with parks on each side that led up to Buckingham Palace.

"This is called the Mall," Malcolm said. "On days like Trooping the Colour—the Queen's official birthday celebration—and other big royal events, people line it on all sides. It's pretty stunning."

Vivian looked around and smiled.

"We have a Mall in our nation's capital, too."

Malcolm glanced over at her with a grin on his face.

"Where do you think you got the idea?"

She continued, as if he hadn't said anything.

"Though ours leads up to a center of democracy, not monarchy."

Malcolm laughed out loud.

"Sometimes, progress isn't all bad."

They got closer to the palace, and Vivian looked up at the enormous stone building. She couldn't believe she was actually going to get to go inside. Malcolm pointed to the top of it.

"No flag—that means, if we had any doubt, that the Queen is not in residence."

"Oh good, I don't have to worry about running into her again. I don't think I'd be able to keep myself from curtsying a second time if we were inside a palace, and my American ego can't handle that."

Malcolm was still laughing as the car slowed, and he . . . Good lord, he just pulled right up to the gates of the palace.

When he said they'd drive there, she'd thought . . . Okay, maybe she hadn't thought about it at all, but she definitely didn't think they would just drive up to the actual gold-tipped ornate gates of actual Buckingham Palace like they belonged there.

But then, she supposed they did.

Vivian looked around, and there was a crowd of people standing by the gates, staring into Malcolm's car. She kept herself—barely—from giving them a beauty pageant wave, and instead looked straight ahead. She couldn't wipe the smile off her face, though.

Malcolm held up his badge to show the guards, and they glanced at it and waved him through.

"I can't believe I was just in a car that drove into Buckingham Palace," she said. "I didn't take any pictures because I didn't want to embarrass you, but please know I wanted to."

He put his hand on hers and smiled at her.

"I'm honored by both parts of that sentence." He lifted her hand and brushed it against his lips. "I'm glad you're enjoying this."

She really wanted to lean over and kiss him, but restrained herself. They were in the parking lot at Buckingham Palace; it didn't seem to be quite the appropriate place for that. She squeezed his hand instead.

"Will there be scones?"

He laughed and turned off the car.

When they walked into the gleaming red, white, and gold state dining room, Vivian stopped and turned around in a circle, her eyes full of wonder.

"All state dinners are held here, as well as other formal dinners," their guide said.

"Wow," Vivian said. She looked overhead. "These chandeliers alone are worth this whole tour. And the ceiling! With the gold accents, it's just stunning."

Malcolm looked around and smiled.

"This place really is so awe-inspiring; it's good for me to stop and remember that."

She'd asked the guide in advance if she could take pictures and had taken a few in every room. He kept waiting for her to take a selfie with him, like she'd done in all of those places in London with her daughter, but she never did.

When they walked out to his car in the palace parking lot over an hour later, she beamed at him.

"Thank you. For arranging that, for letting me spend so much time there, for you and Geraldine answering all of my questions, for everything." Her eyes crinkled, and her smile got sly. "I would kiss you right now for all of that, but I'll wait until we're a safe distance away from the palace."

Before he could help himself, he glanced back toward the palace to see if anyone who knew him was around to hear that, and she laughed out loud.

"I love how tense you get at the mere suggestion of kissing in public. I seem to remember you were a little different on Christmas Eve."

His cheeks got warm when he thought about how he'd kissed her at the party, in full view of anyone who had walked in the dining room.

"That was different. First, it was at a party. Second, there was mistletoe. Third, there was whatever that cocktail was that Julia concocted. There was no possible way for me not to kiss you under all of those circumstances."

He brushed her cheek with his finger, and she smiled up at him.

"Why don't we head over to your flat, so we have some privacy?" she said.

"That's an excellent idea," he said.

He couldn't wait to be alone with her again, so of course it took far longer than usual for him to drive from the palace to his building. He sighed with relief when they finally pulled into the garage.

"Is it unusual to have parking in an apartment building in London?" she asked.

He lifted her suitcase out of the boot of his car.

"Somewhat, and I pay a premium for it," he said. "But there are some days where I need to be able to drive to work." He shrugged. "I was going to make a big thing about how my job is so important and that's why I live here and pay a mint for parking, but really it's because when my marriage split up and I bought this place, I wanted as many conveniences as possible." He led her toward the elevator. "I took this place over another flat that Sarah liked much better, because it had parking, a dishwasher, and a really excellent takeaway curry place right downstairs. Now you know how truly lazy I am."

She slid her arm through his as soon as they got in the elevator, and it took everything in his power not to pull her close.

"We all have our faults, but wanting parking in the building, a dishwasher, and easy access to good curry don't seem like faults to me," she said. "They just make you seem like someone who knows what he likes, that's all."

He looked down at her face, shining up at him.

"I know exactly what I like," he said.

Her cheeks got pink, but she didn't look away.

"So do I," she said.

To hell with it, he could kiss her in this elevator. He should kiss her in this elevator.

Just as he was about to, the elevator doors opened. He

glanced up to see his neighbor looking back at him. He nodded at his neighbor, whose name he'd managed never to discover in his five years living here, and his neighbor nodded back to him. He waited for Vivian to get off the elevator, then led her down the hall to his flat.

"I'm in here," he said as he unlocked his front door. He opened the door for her, and she walked in.

"Wow. Oh wow," she said as she entered his living room. He left her suitcase by the front door and followed her over to the floor-to-ceiling window in the room. "This is incredible," she said.

He put his arm around her and smiled.

"Oh yeah. That was the other reason I took this flat, aside from the dishwasher and the parking."

"And the curry," she reminded him.

"Right, and the curry," he said. "There was also this view."

They stood there together looking out over London. The sun sparkled on the Thames as it wound its path in front of them, alongside landmarks he loved and hated, parts of the city he went to all the time, and parts he'd never visited.

"It's gorgeous." She leaned her head against his shoulder. "How do you not stay here all day, just watching?"

He laughed.

"Luckily for me, it's often very dreary in London, so most of the time when I leave in the morning, I can barely even see the river. But this is another reason I'm pleased the sun was out for you today, so you can see this view in all of its splendor. I hope it's still clear later tonight, when the whole city is lit up."

She smiled up at him.

"Me too."

He couldn't believe he'd finally gotten her back to his flat. They were no longer in public, or on the grounds of his employer, the places they'd been almost the entire time they'd known each other. Even her hotel, as nice as it was, still wasn't actually private. But here, he had her all to himself.

He leaned down to kiss her. She wrapped her arms around his neck and pulled him down to her. She seemed as eager to kiss him, to be here with him, as he was to be with her. Her enthusiasm to spend time with him, to laugh with him, to talk to him, to make love with him, all matched his. He'd almost given up on the possibility of that ever happening.

And she lived over five thousand miles away.

No, that didn't matter right now. She was here with him now, here in his flat now, here, kissing him now; that's what mattered.

He backed her away from the window and fell with her onto his sofa. She laughed as they toppled onto it together.

"Is this what you do, hmm, Mr. Hudson?" She kissed his neck and unbuttoned his top button. "You bring women back to your flat and dazzle them with your incredible view and then tackle them onto the couch?"

Almost never, actually. It was rare for him to click with a woman enough for him to want her in his space. The last few women he'd slept with, he'd gone back to their places, and the relationships hadn't lasted long enough for him to need to invite them over. He'd only had one other date here since he moved into this place, and that had been shortly after he'd moved in; before he realized it was better to keep his home to himself.

"It worked, didn't it?" he said. She laughed and continued to unbutton his shirt.

When they finally surfaced, their clothes were thrown anywhere and everywhere, and they both had very satisfied smiles on their faces.

"You know what?" Vivian said. "I think I like London a whole lot."

"Oh, do you?"

He rolled on top of her and tickled her, just to hear her giggle.

Chapter Eleven

Vivian looked in her suitcase to try to figure out what to wear for her surprise night out with Malcolm. He'd told her to wear something "smart," which was sort of helpful, but not at all as specific as she'd hoped for. If Maddie was around, she would know what "smart" meant to a fifty-something-year-old black British man. But Maddie was back at home, plus Vivian only had a handful of options here in London. Thank goodness she'd overpacked for this trip. She went with a silky magenta wrap dress, black tights and heels, and crossed her fingers that would be both smart enough and warm enough.

After she put her lipstick on, she walked out of the bathroom into the living room to meet Malcolm. When he saw her, he stood up and bowed.

"You look stunning," he said. He took her coat out of his hall closet. "Just incredible."

He held up her coat, and instead of just handing it to her, he helped her put it on. He made her feel so taken care of. It felt unfamiliar and frightening and wonderful.

"Thank you," she said. "You look pretty great, too."

She picked up her new black clutch. Thank God she'd bought it when she and Maddie had done all of that shopping after they'd gotten to London, otherwise she'd be taking her enormous tote bag to wherever they were going tonight.

"Shall we?" He opened the door and gestured for her to precede him.

He seemed so excited about this surprise, but what if she hated whatever it was? Thank God she wasn't afraid of heights, so she didn't have to worry it was dinner on the top of a high building or something. But did he know she was claustrophobic? She should tell him.

"Um, I promise I'm not asking where we're going, but, it's not a tight space, is it? I can be claustrophobic at times—I'm not thrilled with the tiny elevators you have here in London."

He laughed and took her hand as they got out of the elevator.

"I promise, it's not. But if this is making you too worried . . ."

She shook her head.

"No, it's okay. I promise."

She hadn't lied when she'd told Malcolm she trusted him, but that made her nervous, too—how did she have this innate sense of trust for someone she'd known for such a short time?

That's not how she usually was with people. But no matter how much she second-guessed herself about it, the trust was still there between them. She knew it deep down, and she was pretty sure he knew it, too. She was trying not to think about it, or question it too much, but at times she couldn't help herself. The way they'd opened up to each other this morning, how comfortable she'd felt with him all day today—and really ever since they'd first met—how carefree and joyful and just plain great the sex had been . . . It was all like nothing she'd ever experienced. Why was this happening with someone who lived on another continent?

They stood on the street to wait for a taxi, and she made herself shake off all her feelings and just enjoy the night, whatever it ended up being. When the taxi arrived, Malcolm opened the door for her and tucked her coat inside the car with her before closing it again. When he got in next to her, he leaned forward and whispered something to the driver. Then he turned and grinned at her.

"This is killing you. Isn't it?"

She put her head in her hands.

"It's completely killing me, but I'm not going to ask, I swear."

He took her hand as they drove down the busy street.

"Don't worry. You'll know soon enough."

She sighed, then laughed at herself.

"I'm sure you think I'm ridiculous, don't you?"

He squeezed her hand.

"Not at all. I think you're marvelous for letting me surprise you." He lifted her hand and kissed it. "Thank you."

Warmth spread across her chest. She squeezed his hand and released it.

"Thank you for making today so lovely. And I know if I asked, you'd tell me immediately, which I appreciate."

As they drove through London, she saw a few landmarks, but nothing that gave her any hints about where they were going.

Twenty minutes later, the taxi pulled over and stopped. They must be there. Vivian looked outside for a clue. Yet another large, majestic, stone building. Oh yeah, that told her a lot.

Malcolm took her hand again on the sidewalk. Now she knew he was trying to reassure her; this was as much of a public display of affection as Malcolm would ever do (with the exception of that kiss under the mistletoe).

They walked up the steps of the building. Whatever kind of building it was, it looked closed, but she'd already learned things like that weren't a barrier for Malcolm.

Sure enough, the door swung open just as they got to the top.

"Malcolm! Right on time, of course."

A short, round, smiling man with very pale skin and a big dark mustache held the door open for them. Vivian generally had a rule to never trust a man with a mustache, but this one was so adorable she had to smile back at him.

"George, so good to see you, and thanks again. This is my friend, Ms. Vivian Forest, visiting from America. Vivian, this is George Marwick."

Vivian gave George her hand and was briefly convinced he would kiss it. He didn't, but he pressed it between both of his and beamed at her.

"Ms. Forest, welcome to the Victoria and Albert Museum!"

"Thank you so much, it's a joy to be here," she said. Malcolm caught her eye and grinned. She could tell he knew she had no idea what the Victoria and Albert Museum was.

"I believe this is your first visit to the V&A, is that correct, Ms. Forest?" George asked her.

So much so that she hadn't known it existed before, yes.

"Please, call me Vivian," she said. "And yes, it's my first visit here. This is my first trip to England, as a matter of fact."

The little man gasped like she'd given him a special treat.

"Oh, how wonderful! Well, welcome to England in addition to the museum! I hope you've enjoyed your visit?"

She smiled and squeezed Malcolm's hand.

"Tremendously. Thank you so much."

George took off past the vacant check-in desk and beckoned them to follow him.

"Well, that's just glorious. Now, there is so much to see at this museum, but I have orders to take you straight to—" He glanced at Malcolm and then made an exaggerated zipping motion to his lips. "My apologies, my apologies. I don't want to spoil the surprise! Please, just follow me."

What could he be taking her straight to? From some of the signs they passed by, it seemed like this place was full of . . . sculptures? Tapestries? Fashion? Where could they be going?

Had she said something to Malcolm to make him think she loved any of those things?

They followed George through the gift shop, then through a long walkway with a row of sculptures down the middle. She kind of wanted to stop and ask George about the sculptures and why they were here, and if people ever tried to touch them, like she so desperately wanted to do right now, but she could tell Malcolm wanted to get to the surprise.

They went up two flights of wide stone stairs, the last one with a huge painting of a woman at the top. She started to ask George who it was, but she could tell from the excitement on his face that they were almost there.

"This is a real treat you have ahead of you," George said. "All by yourselves in here, when it's usually a mob scene. Just remember, the alarms are all on!"

He chuckled at his joke, and Vivian did, too, even though she had no idea what he was talking about. Just before she followed George through the door, Malcolm leaned down and whispered into her ear.

"I'll be behind you, so you don't have to monitor the look on your face on my account, I promise."

She smiled and stepped inside. She was confused at first. The room was dark, much darker than the rest of the museum. There was no sculpture and no tapestries, just . . .

Oh. My. God.

Jewels.

Everywhere she looked, there were jewels.

She turned in a circle. The room was dark, but there were lights on all of the display cases, and the sparkle was almost blinding. White and red and blue and pink and green and gold, all gleaming out at her.

She looked at Malcolm. He was staring at her and biting his lip.

"You said you hoped to see a tiara in real life."

He'd planned this whole trip, just because she'd said that.

"I can't believe you did this," she said. "You're making me feel like royalty."

A huge smile spread across his face.

"That was the goal," he said. He took her hand. "Come on, George is dying to show you this one."

They walked over to meet George at a small display case halfway into the room.

"There are maybe only five people in the entire United Kingdom I'd do this for," he said, "and Malcolm is one of them."

He carefully put white gloves on and ducked behind the case. Vivian heard a whole series of locks turn. When he came back, the tiara was in his hands.

"This is Queen Victoria's sapphire and diamond coronet," George said. "Her husband Albert designed it for her in 1840. It's been sold a number of times, and almost left England a few years ago, but we managed to get our hands on it, and my goodness were we thrilled about that. We haven't had it in our collection very long, and I'm so happy whenever I look at it. Isn't it a beauty?"

It was a tiny tiara—it almost looked like it had been made for a child—but the jewels in it were huge. The diamonds and sapphires all hit the light and sparkled and shimmered at her.

Vivian tore her eyes away from the tiara and looked at him. "It's stunning. Tiny but incredible."

He beamed at her.

"I'm sorry that I can't allow you to touch it, but . . ."

Vivian shook her head and clasped her hands behind her back.

"Oh my goodness, you have nothing to apologize for. Just letting me look at it like this . . . wow. Thank you so much, George!"

Though . . . she did wish she could try it on.

George smiled at her again, before he put the tiara back in the case and locked it once more. Vivian read the caption about the tiara out loud.

"'It remains an enduring symbol of their love.' Wow, it has a beautiful story, too."

George beamed at her.

"Doesn't it? That's one of the many things I love about it." He looked around and sighed. "Unfortunately, I've got some work to do, so I can't take anything else out of the case, but I'll leave you two here to peruse the rest of the jewelry exhibit. I'll be back in about an hour. I wish I could stay to tell you about everything!" He nodded over to the corner. "Don't mind Lewis over there; he's used to all the oohs and aahs in this room."

Vivian glanced into the corner; she hadn't even noticed the security guard, but of course he'd be there.

George waved at them and disappeared, and she turned to Malcolm.

"I can't believe that happened," she said.

He grinned at her.

"Me neither. Getting in after hours was relatively easy, but when I asked him if there was any way he'd be able to take it out of the case, he hemmed and hawed a lot. I had no idea if he was going to do it until I saw him put the gloves on."

She leaned up and kissed him, security guard be damned.

"I'm so giddy about that, I feel like a little girl going through her princess phase, but I don't even care," she said. "There's so much in this room; I can't wait to look at it all. What a wonderful surprise. Thank you."

"You're very welcome," he said.

She loved how wide the smile on Malcolm's face was.

Malcolm bent down and kissed Vivian before they walked on to see more of the jewels in the exhibit. He'd been worried, ever since she'd told that story about her ex-husband, that she'd feel compelled to fake excitement tonight. And he'd been even more worried that he wouldn't be able to tell if she was excited for real or not. But he'd seen the way her eyes changed when they walked into the museum; he'd been able to tell she was confused and disappointed, even though the smile stayed on her lips. And when they'd walked into this room, he'd seen the wonder and delight and pure joy in them when she realized what surrounded them.

Vivian turned in a circle, her hands still clasped behind her back.

"You always do that with your hands—here, and at Sandringham House, and you did it at Buckingham Palace, too."

She dropped her hands and laughed.

"Oh, that's because I always desperately want to touch things in museums! I have to hold my hands together behind my back so I won't be tempted."

Malcolm laughed and took hold of her hand.

"Here we go. I'll keep you from temptation."

They spent the next hour and a half—George always had been a softy—walking around the exhibit, reading about everything there, and making quiet fun of some of the ugliest of the jewels.

"Some people really do have more money than sense," Vivian said. "Why would you do that to those poor jewels?"

Malcolm laughed.

"Can you imagine actually wearing that thing? It would frighten children on the street!"

Vivian chuckled again. He loved that throaty laugh of hers—it seemed to bubble up out of nowhere and was so full of joy that it always made him laugh, too.

"On the other hand, that tiara is just majestic. It looks really heavy, but it's gorgeous."

She leaned her head against his shoulder, and he put his

arm around her. They stood there like that for a while, until she turned toward him.

"Thank you for doing this for me," she whispered, her hand on his cheek.

"Thank you for letting me do this for you," he whispered back. And then he kissed her. He didn't care that George would be back any second, or that video cameras were definitely on them, or that the security guard in the corner was watching them; all he cared about was her lips on his, her body against his, her breath melding with his.

Finally, they broke apart. He almost felt ridiculous about how much he was smiling, but he was too happy to do anything else. He reached for her hand.

"We ought to go soon; George has given us far more time than I asked for, and now I feel guilty about keeping him at work this late the week after Christmas."

"No need to feel guilty!" George bounced over to them. "I'm going on holiday for three weeks in January; I needed to stay late anyway to get all of my work in order. Lost track of time tonight, but I'm sure you two made good use of it."

Vivian looked around the room as they left it, almost like she was bidding the jewels farewell.

"We did. This exhibit is wonderful, and I can't thank you enough for giving us this time with it. I enjoyed it so much." She glanced from side to side as they walked out into the hallway. "I'm only upset we didn't get a chance to see anything else in the museum. If this exhibit is here, I can only imagine what other surprises this place has in store."

How did Vivian always know the exact right thing to say to everyone? George almost embraced her. He loved this museum so much, bless him.

"Would you like to see some of them? We have time for . . ." George looked at his watch, and his face fell. "Oh no, I'm supposed to meet my wife at nine, and it's twenty to. Well, we have time to just walk through one of my favorite exhibits here."

He took off at a trot. Malcolm hid his grin as they hurried to catch up with George. Good thing he'd made their dinner reservation for half past nine, even though their appointment with George was at seven. He knew George far too well to think he wouldn't get distracted by his museum. He was certain George's wife wasn't counting on him meeting her at nine, either.

Finally, after a jaunt through exhibits about mosaics, glass, and dollhouses (all surprisingly fascinating), George waved good-bye to them at the door.

"Ms. Forest—Vivian—it's been a real pleasure. I certainly hope you make it back to London for a proper visit to the V&A. And Malcolm, it was lovely to see you again."

Vivian reached for his hand.

"George, thank you so much for everything. This was wonderful. I enjoyed myself so much."

He pumped her hand with both of his and held on for so long that Malcolm wondered if he should be jealous.

"It was truly my honor," George said. "See you again, I hope."

She slipped her arm into Malcolm's as they waited for a taxi, and he pulled her close.

"Oh, Malcolm," she said, "that may have been the best surprise I've ever had in my life." She sighed, a smile still on her lips. "I know I keep saying it, but thank you."

He leaned down and kissed her softly on the lips.

"You don't have to keep thanking me; that smile on your face is all the thanks I need," he said. He opened the taxi door for her. "Now, let's see if we make our half past nine dinner reservation before the restaurant gives up on us."

Luckily, they only ended up about ten minutes late, and after profuse apologies, the host seated them.

"I don't think there's going to be the same kind of show tonight as there was last night," Malcolm said. "This place isn't known for its spicy food, but it is very well known for its Israeli food, and it's delicious."

She looked down at the menu.

"I think Maddie's boyfriend has one of the cookbooks from this place. Everything in it looks delicious and very complicated to make." She smiled at him. "I'm glad someone else is making it for me."

He was so happy with how their day had gone, and so hungry from how late it was, that he ordered half the menu.

"I didn't want to rush you out of the museum, but my stomach was starting to rumble by the end there," he said when their wine arrived.

She laughed.

"Mine did, too, but I was having so much fun with George,

I didn't want to leave!" She lifted her glass of wine. "To George, the first person in a long time who has made me forget how hungry I was!"

He touched his glass to hers.

"To George!"

"I love museums, and I never go enough," she said. "Whenever I travel anywhere, I visit a ton of museums, but I go to maybe one every two years at home, which makes no sense. We have so many wonderful museums in the Bay Area, but between work and everything else it never occurs to me to go when I'm at home."

He nodded.

"I used to go a lot with Miles—Sarah has never really cared about art, and I was the one who introduced him to the work of a lot of his favorite painters." He sighed. "Which is one of the many reasons why Sarah is so angry at me because of this. Mind you, I'm also the one who got him excited about going to Oxford, too, but that doesn't really matter now."

Vivian put her hand on his.

"You haven't heard from him?"

Malcolm shook his head. Not a text, not a phone call.

"Have you reached out to him?"

He shook his head again and sighed. He'd managed to put the whole mess with Miles out of his mind for most of the day.

"I'm still just so angry. At him, at his ridiculous instructor who put these dreams into his head and told him to apply to art school of all things instead of going to Oxford, at myself. I should have done a better job, throughout the years, teaching him the realities of life. How important it is to get certain credentials, how—especially for people who look like us—it smooths out so much and opens so many doors for the rest of your life." He sighed. "I suppose at some point I should reach out to him and try to talk sense into him again. You may have a point."

She sipped her wine.

"I wasn't making a point. I was just asking a question."

His eyebrows went up.

"You can't trick me with that 'I was just asking a question' social worker move, Ms. Forest. I've been working in and around government far too long for that; I know pointed questions from pointed questions."

She laughed.

"Sorry, I can't help it. I've been a social worker for over twenty years; some things are just part of me now." Now she raised her eyebrows at him. "Do you not want to talk about this right now? We can talk about something else that doesn't involve me prying into your psyche."

He grinned.

"You weren't prying, but let's talk about you instead of me. Tell me more about this big-deal new job you're about to step into."

No wonder Vivian worried about her facial expressions showing too much. He could tell just from the way her smile faded at that question that she had mixed feelings about the job.

"Well, starting in February, I'll be the interim director of social work at the hospital. And if I get the permanent job—which, from what my boss says, is a shoo-in, but I'm trying not to count my chickens before they're hatched—I'll be the director of social work."

"How is that different from what you're doing now?" he asked.

She took a deep breath.

"It's some of what I'm doing now, just a lot more of it, and more of other things, too. Right now I do mostly patient work—talking through diagnoses and worries with patients after they see their doctors, helping them access services both inside and outside of the hospital, working with their families. This is the hardest and most rewarding part of the job for me, especially when the patient is a child or teenager. My boss does a little of that, too, but mostly only if there's a major problem, or if we're short-staffed or something. And of course, when there's a crisis. Otherwise, it's a lot of managing people, working with the big bosses at the hospital, working with other hospitals and local agencies, that kind of stuff. A lot of responsibilities I don't have now."

He touched her hand.

"I'm positive you'll do it all very well."

She nodded quickly.

"Oh, sure. I'm not worried about that. It's just"—she shrugged—"I guess I hadn't realized how much I like my current job until it was time to leave it. That's all."

He almost asked her if she was sure she wanted this new job. But she seemed so set on it, that it felt like a ridiculous question.

"Well, it's my job now to make sure you have a fantastic holiday while you're here. What should we do tomorrow? Do you want to see the crown jewels? And before you ask, there's no way those will get taken out of the case."

She laughed out loud.

"I wouldn't have asked! But then, I wouldn't have asked for tonight, either."

She smiled at him over her wineglass. He suddenly couldn't wait to get her home.

Chapter Twelve

Vivian woke up the next morning and listened to the sounds of London out the window. Even from this high up, she could hear the early morning noises of the city—the swish of the rain, honks from cars, the occasional siren as it went by. She loved how even the sounds of London felt different than the sounds of California; yes, the sirens were different, but it felt like something else, too. She was so glad she'd gotten to experience this.

She turned over in Malcolm's large and comfortable bed. It was so big they'd been able to sleep far enough apart that she didn't feel crowded, but close enough so she could feel his body heat. She pulled the duvet up to her shoulders in the chill of the room. They'd said it was so cold at Sycamore Cottage because it was an old house, but Malcolm's building seemed pretty new and up-to-date, yet it was cold here, too. Maybe homes were just that cold everywhere in England.

She looked down at herself and grinned. Or maybe it was because she'd slept naked. No wonder she was colder than normal.

"What are you smiling to yourself about?"

She turned, and Malcolm was looking at her, with his head propped up on his hand.

"Oh. I didn't know you were awake," she said.

He scooted closer to her and put his arm around her.

"Hmm, interesting that you didn't answer the question. Ever heard that doing that just makes people more eager to hear the answer, Ms. Forest?"

She didn't quite look him in the eye. She'd had sex with him, multiple times at this point, so why was she so embarrassed to say this to him?

"I was just thinking that it was cold in here," she said, still looking down at the blankets. "And then that maybe it was so cold because I don't have any clothes on, which isn't how I normally sleep. That's all."

He kissed her shoulder.

"'Normally'?"

She rolled her eyes.

"Fine. Never. Happy?"

He rubbed his hand up and down her arm.

"Very happy, as a matter of fact." He kissed her collarbone.

"Come to think about it, you do feel chilly. But I'm honored that you slept naked for me. Or maybe I distracted you too much for you to get up and put something on before you went to sleep, like you did at the hotel?"

She tried to fight back her grin.

"Maybe," she said.

He rolled over on top of her and kissed the hollow between her breasts.

"Well, since it's my fault you're cold this morning, I see it as my duty to warm you up. Luckily, I can think of a good way to do that."

An hour later, she was in his kitchen making them both tea. Thank goodness he had a big, cozy robe for her to wear over her pajamas, otherwise she'd probably stay in bed with him for hours.

Actually . . . that didn't sound so bad.

He padded into the kitchen with sweatpants on.

"We got those pastries yesterday when we were out; I thought we could warm them up in the oven for breakfast?"

She opened the oven to show him the pastries inside and on a cookie sheet.

"I got that far, but I couldn't quite figure out how to turn on your oven. I kept pressing buttons that beeped angrily at me, and I finally gave up."

He laughed and reached over her.

"You have to push these two buttons at the same time; I know it's ridiculous, but I'm used to it at this point."

Ten minutes later, as they sat at his kitchen table with a

plate of warm pastries in front of them and full mugs of tea, Vivian heard a key in his front door.

"Um, Malcolm?" She gestured toward the door, and he jumped up.

"Probably just building maintenance. Excuse me."

But before he could get to the door, it opened, and a young, tall, brown-skinned man walked in.

"Oh." He stopped when he saw Malcolm. "I didn't realize you'd be home."

"Miles!" Malcolm walked toward him. "What are you doing here?"

The boy's lips were tight, and he didn't look at Malcolm.

"I just came to return this." He held up the key. "I obviously won't be needing it anymore."

Malcolm's eyes narrowed.

"Now, Miles, don't you think—"

Vivian stood up. It was well past time for her to intervene.

"Hi, Miles. I'm Vivian," she said. "We have a full pot of tea and some pastries here. Would you like some?"

He looked from Malcolm to her and then back to Malcolm.

"Oh. I didn't realize . . ."

She didn't wait for him to answer her and poured him a mug. "How do you take your tea, Miles? I know your uncle likes it with nothing in it, but I like a little cream and sugar both in mine."

He hesitated. He was clearly too polite to reject her offer, thank goodness. And thank God Malcolm had the good sense to keep his mouth shut.

"Sugar, please. About a spoonful?" He hesitated, then walked over to her. "I'm sorry, have we met?"

She stirred the sugar into his tea and shook her head.

"We haven't, but I've been hoping to meet you. I'm a friend of your uncle's, visiting from the States." She handed him the mug.

"I thought you sounded American! Where do you live? I've always wanted to visit New York." He took a sip of the tea.

She smiled at him and went around to the table.

"Come, sit down and have a pastry. We got them yesterday at this great bakery in—what neighborhood was that in, Malcolm?"

"Soho," Malcolm said, as he sat down next to her.

"Yes, there. It's my first time in London—I keep forgetting where I am."

Miles walked over to the table to look at the plate full of pastries. See? She knew you had to lure teenage boys with food. Worked every time.

"And I'm from California, not New York, but I've been to New York a few times, and always have a wonderful time whenever I go. Though"—she made a face—"I can't handle it there in the summer. I've only been during the summer once, but never again. So hot and sticky and there's garbage every-where." She picked up her tea. "Then again, I still had a great time even in the heat; the museums are fantastic, and my God, the food is good. You should definitely go as soon as you can."

Miles plopped down across the table from her and picked up a bun.

"Oh yeah, I really want to! But California seems amazing,

too—so different from London. What are you . . . ?" He glanced at Malcolm and quickly looked back at her. "How long have you been in London?"

What a polite child he was. He was clearly dying to know what the hell this woman he'd never heard of was doing in his uncle's kitchen, but he wouldn't let himself ask. She'd take pity on him.

"I've just been in London for a few days, but I've been in England for a little bit over a week. My daughter and I were here for Christmas visiting some of her friends, and after Christmas we came to London, and I've been here since then." She didn't need to tell him the *whole* story. "I've had a fantastic time so far, though I hadn't realized just how different England and America were until my time here. Even our words for food are so different."

Miles burst out laughing.

"It's so true! One time, this kid from the States was in my school because his mum was working here—he got so confused when someone said we had flapjacks. He thought they would be pancakes!"

Vivian looked at him sideways.

"Okay, now you're going to have to explain this to me; what *are* flapjacks? I would definitely think that was a pancake."

Malcolm broke in.

"I believe you'd call them granola bars, or something close to them?"

Vivian laughed.

"I'd be confused, too."

Miles grinned at her.

"The kid in my school was very confused." He reached for another pastry. "What's California like? Are there really palm trees everywhere like on TV?"

Vivian laughed.

"Not quite everywhere, but we do have our fair share of palm trees. I live in Northern California, so it's not quite as warm and beachy, but still warmer than"—she gestured to the windows—"this."

He eagerly asked her more questions about California, New York, and other places in America, and she answered them as well as she could. She steered the conversation away from both art and universities as much as possible, and she didn't think Miles noticed. At one point, Malcolm put his hand on her thigh and squeezed, and she covered it with her own.

"Okay, is it true that—" Miles broke off and pulled his phone out of his pocket. "Oh damn." He looked up at her. "Sorry, I mean . . ."

She laughed.

"Miles, I've heard 'damn' before, it's okay. Is something wrong?"

He stood up.

"Yes. I mean no. I mean it's just I was supposed to meet my girlfriend a quarter of an hour ago. I have to go."

She walked over to the door with him.

"Well, I don't want to keep you. But I'm so glad I got a chance to meet you, and I hope you have a very happy New Year."

He smiled at her and reached out to shake her hand. She was about to lean in for a hug, but okay, she'd shake hands instead.

"It was great to meet you, too, Ms. . . . Vivian." He glanced at Malcolm, who she could feel behind her, and back at her. "Bye."

"Bye, Miles," they both said, as he walked out the door.

They were silent until they heard the elevator ding. Then they looked at each other and laughed.

"How did you do that?" he asked her. "He was all geared up for another fight when he walked in here, I could tell. And you just . . . gave him tea and offered him pastries and got him to sit down and relax?"

She grinned at him.

"I've had lots of practice in making friends with surly teenage boys—and girls." She picked up her mug and took a sip. "I just figured the two of you needed a little time-out where you could relax around each other so you could both find a way to put your weapons down. I'm glad I could help." She cocked an eyebrow at him. "And did you notice that he forgot to leave your key here?"

Malcolm jumped up and looked at the counter, then turned around and stared at her.

"I didn't even realize that. Vivian, I may need to break into the glass today—I think you deserve to wear some of the crown jewels just for that!"

She stood up and fluffed her hair.

"Well, I'd better go get ready for that, then. I don't want to be late for my coronation!"

What would have happened if Vivian hadn't been there? Malcolm wondered. Would he and Miles have had another fight? Would Miles have just thrown the key at him and left again? One thing was for sure: they definitely wouldn't have made up. The stony expression on Miles's face every time he'd looked at him had told him that.

Though . . . there were a few times, when they were all sitting at the table together talking about travel and U.S./British relations and everything else, where Miles had looked at him like he'd used to, like they were sharing a joke.

He wanted to get that back for good.

Midway through their tour of the Tower of London, Vivian looked at him.

"You need to apologize to Miles, you know."

What? She'd taken *that* from what he'd told her?

"The hell I do," he said. He stopped himself and shook his head. "I'm sorry. I shouldn't have said that. What I meant was . . ."

She laughed.

"Oh, I know what you meant—you meant what you said. But I meant what I said, too. This fight with Miles is killing you, I can tell. I've only known you a little over a week, and I know he's the most important relationship in your life. You can't destroy it like this; you and I both know that. Apologize to the boy. Talk to him. Ask him questions about why he wants to do this."

He dropped his hand from her back. He thought she would be on his side here.

"I know why he wants to do this! Because he has this youthful infatuation with the idea of being an artist, and he hasn't thought it all through!"

Vivian nodded slowly.

"That's one perspective. But you told me Miles said he feels like he needs to be passionate about this, that he doesn't want to waste any moment of life, that he's feeling his own mortality because his father died young—I'm not saying I agree with him, but after seeing what my sister has gone through, I understand what he's saying. Talk this over with him; he's obviously really thought about it. See if you can come to some sort of common ground. But don't just expect him to bow to your will."

This is what came of opening yourself up to people. He never should have told her about their conversation in that much detail.

"I'm not expecting him to bow to my will. I'm simply expecting him to act like an adult. He needs to listen to the people who know better about what he should do with his life. I'm not going to apologize to a nineteen-year-old for calling him ridiculous for wanting to go to art school instead of Oxford!"

She nodded.

"Okay, great. And where's that gotten you so far?"

He turned away from her.

"You don't understand. Just because you spent thirty minutes talking to Miles doesn't mean you know him. Or me."

She opened her mouth, then closed it.

"Okay. That's certainly one way to respond."

They were silent for the rest of the tour.

He checked his phone on the way out and saw an email he really should respond to.

He cleared his throat and turned to Vivian.

"Would you mind terribly if we went back to my apartment now? There's some work I should get done this afternoon. I can order in for lunch, if you're hungry."

She shook her head slowly.

"I don't mind at all, and I'm not hungry quite yet. I can read while you work; I'm excited to get back to my book."

When they returned to his apartment, he fetched his computer from his messenger bag, where it had been ever since he'd gotten back from Sandringham. He sat at the corner of the couch. Vivian made another pot of tea and poured him some, without asking him if he wanted any. She sat in his easy chair, instead of on the couch with him, with a book and her own cup of tea.

She was wrong about what she'd said about Miles. She was obviously wrong about it. Why should he apologize to Miles? Miles was the one who was destroying his life. Miles was the one who had insulted him! He'd spent years helping him and indulging him and preparing him, and they'd gotten there, he'd gotten into Oxford, then Miles wanted to go and throw that away. He had nothing to apologize for.

He tried to bury himself in work, but it only took about ten minutes to respond to that email, and as much as he tried to focus on other tasks, Vivian's presence across from him made it impossible for him to concentrate. Which in turn frustrated him—he'd used work as his distraction for years. Why wasn't it working today?

He sighed and looked at Vivian, then away. He was still upset with her for what she'd said about him and Miles, remember?

He had yelled at the boy, though. And laughed at him. And told him he was acting like a child, when Malcolm knew he most wanted to be treated as an adult.

But even so! What was he supposed to do—go to Miles with his hat in hand and tell him he was doing everything right and he was sorry he'd ever questioned him? That was impossible.

But he hated that he'd snapped at Vivian and made everything awkward between them again. Even though he didn't agree with her advice, she was just trying to help.

"I'm sorry," he said out of the blue.

Vivian put a finger in her book and looked at him.

He closed his computer and put it on the coffee table.

"I'm sorry I was so rude to you. And I'm sorry I said what I did about you not knowing me—that was both unkind and untrue. I just don't know what to do here."

Vivian put her book down on the table.

"I know it wasn't my place to give you advice about what to do with Miles. But I also know you're so upset about this, and he seems like such a good kid—I don't want this to cause a permanent rift between the two of you."

He rubbed his forehead.

"Me neither." He wished he could go back to Christmas Eve, when everything was relaxed and easy and he thought Miles's big news was that he was going to move in with his girlfriend. "And you're right, I am so upset about this. But that's no excuse for how I treated you this morning. I shouldn't have been quite so . . ."

"Cold and British?" she filled in.

He laughed.

"That's one way to put it." They smiled at each other. He was so relieved she was smiling back at him. Why had he wasted precious time quarreling with her? Especially since the last thing he wanted was for Vivian to be angry with him. "And I'm sorry I've been such a boor all afternoon." He took a sip of his now-cold tea. "Vivian, I don't want to apologize to him. I hate this, I hate that he's doing this, it makes me furious, and I can't tell him he's doing everything right, because he isn't. I just wish he would listen to me."

Vivian nodded.

"I know."

He got up and put the kettle on for more tea, and went back to the couch.

"I don't know how to talk to him about this. Passion doesn't put a roof over your head or food on your table. Do you think

I had a lifelong passion to work for the Queen? No—I realized early on what I was good at and where I would thrive, then I worked to make it happen. I didn't spend years pretending the monarchy was my top priority out of passion; I did it because I was strategic about my career. His love for art is all well and good, but I wish he would be realistic."

Vivian moved over to the couch and sat next to him.

"Hey." She moved her hand up to the back of his neck and rubbed the tight muscles there. "That part is okay. What he wants to do isn't what you or I would do, that's for sure. But you don't have to approve of everything he's doing to start a dialogue with him about why he's doing it."

He nodded as he relaxed against her strong fingers.

"You're right. But . . ."

She shook her head.

"I know you don't want to apologize for how you reacted on Christmas. But he's a proud kid, and you mocked him for his dreams." He started to respond to that, but she put her finger on his lips. "I know you didn't do it on purpose, but don't you think that's how he sees it?"

He nodded again.

"You're probably right about that." He put his arm around her. "I'm sorry you're in the middle of all of this. You only have a few days left in London, and I've involved you in my family drama."

She kissed him on the cheek.

"Don't worry about it. When I take the new job, I won't be in the trenches in family dramas anymore; I'm going to miss it."

He laughed and pulled her closer.

"Now that I've helped you have a bit of a busman's holiday, we should make the most of our remaining time together."

She raised an eyebrow at him.

"Did you have something specific in mind, Mr. Hudson?"

He whispered in her ear. She let out that explosive giggle again, right before he kissed her.

Chapter Thirteen

Vivian woke up on New Year's Eve and held back a sigh. It felt like Sunday night and the last night of summer vacation, all rolled into one. The next day, she would fly back to California, and this surprising, magical, unprecedented interlude would be over. She would be back to everyday Vivian, the one who didn't get to wander around a city on a whim, the one who didn't go to museums often, even when they interested her, the one who didn't go out with men very much, even though she wanted to.

She opened her eyes and looked at Malcolm. He was still sound asleep. She wanted to reach out and trace the smile lines around his mouth, and his slightly pouty bottom lip, but he looked so peaceful she didn't want to wake him up.

She was going to miss him. Yes, she would miss the England Vivian, who was carefree and had decided not to worry about her new job until she got home, who thought about having fun and not what was prudent or checked all the right boxes, who made snap decisions instead of weighing pros and cons. But she would also really miss Malcolm. She'd clicked with him in a way she hadn't clicked with anyone in years—not just romantically, but as a person. They laughed at the same things, they cared about the same things, and when they had a conflict, one or the other of them would give the other a metaphorical shake, and they'd figure it out. How had they managed to figure out how to fight well together in less than two weeks?

She shook her head, and a sigh finally escaped her. His eyes immediately popped open, and she laughed.

"I thought you were still asleep," she said.

He put an arm around her and pulled her close. She leaned her head against his shoulder. They even agreed on the correct way to sleep—with just enough space between the two of them so they could sense the other one was there, but never enough to touch during the night. She loved being held by him and the way he touched her, and she was so glad he never did it while she was trying to sleep.

"What do you want to do today, on our last full day?" he asked.

She looked over at him—and marveled that his face was already so familiar to her. The creases around his lips when he smiled, those tiny freckles along his cheekbones, the cleft in his chin, the gray hairs in his morning stubble.

"I just want to spend time with you," she said.

His smile dazzled her.

"That's exactly what I want to do, too." He pursed his lips together, then held up a finger. "I have a tiny surprise in store for later, but if you want to know what it is . . ."

She laughed. Of course he had.

"Your first surprise was so good that now I have no choice but to say yes. You know that, right?"

He brushed his finger against her cheek.

"That's so kind of you to say, but really, I'm happy to tell you if you want."

She shook her head. She had no idea what had gotten into her during this trip, but now she was actually looking forward to his surprise.

"Nope. As long as it's not going to some huge New Year's Eve party, or standing outside to watch the London equivalent of the ball dropping, I'm okay."

He shuddered.

"I promise you, it's definitely neither of those things, nor anything like them, as a matter of fact."

She smiled and kissed his cheek.

"Perfect."

He bent down to kiss her, and she pulled him closer.

"Mmm, just one question," she said after a few minutes. "Just so I'm clear—is this your surprise?"

He ran his hand down her body and sucked her bottom lip into his mouth before answering. As it happened, when he did that, she no longer cared what his response might be.

"This is just the first thing on the agenda," he finally said. "Well, it might be the fourth thing, too, and possibly the eighth thing, and definitely the last thing, but not the only thing."

She laughed and kissed his shoulder.

"Like I said, whatever your plan is, I'm in."

Malcolm went into the kitchen while Vivian finished getting dressed. He couldn't wipe the smile from his face when he thought of what they'd already done that morning, and of spending the whole day with her today.

And tomorrow, she would leave. That thought gave him a lump in the pit of his stomach. No, he couldn't think about that right now; he was going to concentrate on today. He turned over the bacon in the pan and poured out their coffee, just as Vivian came out of the bedroom.

"I made us a quick breakfast," he said. "Just toast and coffee and bacon, but don't worry, I have good ideas for food for later."

She picked up her coffee cup and grinned over it at him.

"I wasn't worried," she said. She sat down at the table and took a sip of coffee.

He brought the food and his coffee over to the table and joined her.

"Traffic and parking are going to be a nightmare today, so I thought we'd take the tube everywhere."

She took a bite of toast and nodded.

"Do you know what I haven't done yet . . . ?" She shook her head and trailed off. "No, never mind, there's a lot I haven't done yet, and I only have one more day, so it doesn't matter."

He put his coffee cup down.

"What if you told me anyway, though?" This was slightly dangerous; suppose she brought up going to Windsor or Wimbledon or somewhere else that would take the whole day? But he still had to ask.

She looked up at him, a sheepish smile on her face.

"I haven't ridden on the top of one of those red buses. I know, it's so dorky, but I've seen pictures of them my whole life, and Maddie and I were going to do it, but we ran out of time . . ."

Now this, he could manage.

"That's easy. And I haven't done that in a while, either. It'll be a treat for me, too."

The smile that spread across her face made him so happy, he knew he would have said yes, no matter what she'd asked for.

Thirty minutes later, they were on the upper deck of a bus, with very few other people.

Vivian looked around and grinned as they trundled through London.

"I still can't believe these are just the normal way people get around this city. They're so cool." She pulled her phone out of her pocket. "I don't care if it makes us look like tourists; I'm going to make you take a selfie with me."

He groaned, but he couldn't keep the smile from his face.

"If we must. It is your last day, after all."

She handed him her phone.

"Your arms are longer. You take it."

He put his arm around her shoulders and angled the camera to get some of London going by in the background. They both smiled into the phone for the photo, then—maybe because he'd been overcome by sentiment when he'd said, "last day," he took her by surprise and kissed her on the cheek. She let out a giggle just as he took the picture.

"There." He handed the phone back to her. "Are you happy?"

She nodded.

"Very." She looked at the photos and smiled up at him. "Are you?"

He touched her cheek with his thumb.

"Absolutely." He gestured to her phone. "Send those to me, won't you?" he asked her.

She grinned and nodded.

They decided to go to the Tate Modern, mostly because it was on this bus route. After a few hours of culture, they headed to Borough Market, an outdoor covered marketplace with tons of stalls selling different kinds of food. Vivian's eyes widened as they walked inside, and he grinned. He knew she'd like it here.

"I thought we'd have dinner at my apartment tonight, since anywhere we went would be a madhouse. We can eat lunch here, then pick up all sorts of supplies for tonight," he said.

"That sounds perfect," she said.

They wandered around the whole market and stopped at stalls that sold cheese, charcuterie, bread, jam, chocolates, oysters, and all sorts of meat pies, and bought all the above and then some. They ate until they were bursting, and then bought cake for dessert.

The tube ride back home was unusually boisterous. Most of the time, Londoners didn't interact with one another on public transportation, but there were too many excited people on there for it to be a normal day. Okay, excited wasn't quite the right word; most of them seemed half-drunk already, but in the happy, giggly way, which made both him and Vivian laugh, too.

When they walked into his apartment, Vivian helped him put the food away, then threw herself on the couch.

"I can't bring myself to regret that last sausage roll," she said, "even though it might kill me."

He lay down next to her. Thank goodness this couch was roomy.

"My problem was the dumplings. They were delicious, but did I need all twelve?"

They looked at each other and laughed.

"Yes, obviously, you did," she said.

Later that afternoon, they took a sunset walk down to the Thames. Vivian would never get over how early sunset was here at this time of year. It was also very cold, but between how well she was bundled up and Malcolm's warm hand in hers, she didn't care.

Despite how dark it was this early, she couldn't remember

the last time she'd been this happy. It obviously wasn't just Malcolm, but he'd made this vacation such a dream—so relaxing, and fun, and interesting. And the way he looked at her sometimes . . . well, those parts had been an added delight.

When they got back to his apartment, she immediately shed all of her outer layers, then paused and stared at her half-packed suitcase. Malcolm came out of the bathroom and saw her standing there.

"Something wrong, V?" he asked.

She liked the way he'd started to call her V. Her family called her Viv, which she hated from anyone outside of her family. But she liked V from him a lot.

She shook her head at his question.

"No, nothing wrong."

He came over to her.

"Okay, but you're looking indecisive about something. What is it?"

Sometimes it was annoying that he was so perceptive.

"It's nothing bad . . . I was just wondering if . . ."

She felt silly about this, but then, he hadn't found any of her quirks silly yet.

"Since it's New Year's Eve, should I change? Into something more fun, I mean." She had no idea why she'd suddenly felt the need to change, but for some reason, she really wanted to.

A wide smile spread across Malcolm's face.

"What a smashing idea. Absolutely, you should change. We should both change. Let's do that, then open the first bottle of champagne."

She grinned at him, plucked a dress out of her suitcase, and disappeared into the bathroom. After twenty minutes, most of which was spent putting her hair in as fancy an updo as she could manage, and using that sparkly eye makeup Maddie had given her, she emerged.

"Just warning you now; you've already seen this dress before," she said as she stepped out of the bathroom.

He turned around, midway through tying his bow tie.

"I loved it on Christmas Eve, and I love it even more on New Year's Eve," he said. "You look incredible." He bent down to kiss her, and she wrapped her arms around his neck and kissed him back hard.

"Let's pop that first bottle of champagne."

She followed him into the kitchen. He pulled a bottle out of the fridge and carefully took down two champagne glasses from the cabinet. He paused before he opened the bottle and smiled at her.

"Confession: I just bought these glasses a few days ago, once I realized you'd be here with me on New Year's Eve. I haven't had a reason to have champagne glasses in this apartment until now."

He unwound the wire around the cork and pulled the cork out with a gentle pop. After he'd filled their glasses, she lifted her glass to his.

"To both of us having more reasons to drink champagne."

He grinned at her.

"What a perfect toast."

They spent the next few hours sitting on the couch talking,

drinking champagne, and looking out over London. After a while they both got hungry, so he got up and shucked the oysters they'd bought at the market. Later they got even hungrier, so she made them an enormous cheese plate with the many different kinds of cheese and charcuterie they'd bought earlier that day. And then, when they wanted something sweet, he served them slices of the chocolate cake they'd bought. And with everything, they drank more champagne.

At one point, he reached over and took her hand.

"I wish . . ." he said, and trailed away.

She wasn't sure his wish was exactly the same as hers— that they had more time together, that they lived in the same city, that they could suspend time for minutes or hours or days until they could get their fill of each other—but she recognized the look in his eyes as the same feeling in her heart.

"I do, too," she said.

He sighed and pulled her closer to him.

"I hoped you did," he said.

A few minutes before midnight, Malcolm brought a new bottle of champagne to the coffee table and popped the cork.

"And the New Year is just seconds away," he said, as he poured champagne into both of their glasses. He looked at his watch. "Ten . . . nine . . . eight . . . seven . . ."

Vivian joined him in the countdown.

". . . three . . . two . . . one!" they said in unison. They turned to each other and smiled.

"Happy New Year, Vivian," he said.

"Happy New Year, Malcolm," she said.

She started to clink her glass against his, but he shook his head.

"You're forgetting the most important thing about midnight at the New Year," he said. "The kiss."

She was forgetting that, as a matter of fact. How many years had it been since she'd had someone to kiss on New Year's Eve? She'd certainly kissed people on New Year's Eve, but it had been quite a while since she was guaranteed a kiss on that night. And from a person she truly wanted to kiss.

He took her glass from her and put it down onto the coffee table, then swept her into a kiss that left her breathless. When they finally parted, he brushed her hair back from her face and kissed her cheek.

"Now we toast." He handed her the champagne glass and picked up his own.

She touched her glass to his.

"Happy New Year. I hope this year ends as well as it began."

He lifted his glass to his lips.

"Well, I can definitely toast to that." A wide smile crossed his face. "And you said that without even seeing the one last surprise I had in store for you."

She narrowed her eyes at him. She'd forgotten about his last surprise. Did he think she was in any shape to leave his apartment again tonight, with all this champagne they'd had? Or had he bought her a present?

He laughed out loud.

"I see that look on your face; no need to be so suspicious. I can't take credit for this, but I love it anyway. Look!" He gestured in front of them at the windows, and she turned to look at what he could be talking about. At first there was nothing, but then:

Fireworks!

They exploded right in front of her, it felt like. Huge white cartwheels of fireworks, bright red pinwheels, sparkling gold fizzy ones. She turned back to him with her eyes wide open.

"Oh my goodness! I can't believe you get this amazing show, right here on your couch!"

He put his arm around her and pulled her close, as they both stared at the colors lighting up the night sky out the window.

"Me neither, honestly. I didn't even know I got this view until my first New Year's Eve here. That was"—he shook his head—"a pretty lonely night, to be honest. I'd told myself I was going to go to bed early and not even bother with midnight or any of that, but I couldn't sleep, so I wandered out into the kitchen to get a snack just before midnight, and when I turned around, this was right outside the window. I sat down and stared in wonder." She took his hand and squeezed it, and he leaned down to kiss her cheek. "It's nice to share this view with someone."

She turned and smiled up at him.

"I'm so happy I get to share it with you."

They watched the fireworks in silence for a while, then suddenly, Malcolm dropped his arm from her shoulder and turned to face her.

"Okay, but seriously. What if we keep this up?"

Vivian let her heart soar for a brief moment, before she

forced herself back to earth. This had all felt like a miracle—
a jewel of a week that would sparkle in her memory for years
to come—but this wasn't real life. She wasn't some twenty-
year-old in a movie who went to a foreign country and fell in
love; people like her didn't get swept up in fairy tales.

"We're a little too old for long-distance relationships, don't
you think?" she said.

He laughed.

"God yes, that seems way too complicated and difficult.
I'm definitely far too old and conservative for something like
that. Just . . . we'd visit each other occasionally and have a
week like this, then both go back to our regular lives."

Oh. Of course that's what he meant. That made sense.

Vivian made herself laugh.

"So you want a long-distance booty call? I'm definitely too
old—and conservative—for that."

Malcolm dropped his eyes and put his champagne glass
down.

"I wouldn't have phrased it in quite that way . . ."

She patted him on the shoulder.

"I know you wouldn't have, but I did."

Plus—and she couldn't tell him this part—she knew she'd
gotten far too attached to Malcolm in the week and a half she'd
known him. It would be fine; she knew she'd get over it after a
while once she was at home and he wasn't around. But also she
knew herself well enough to know that if she and Malcolm
stayed in contact in the way he'd suggested, her feelings would
just grow stronger. And it would hurt more once it ended.

She took his hand.

"This was a perfect week, and I'm so grateful to you for it."

He picked up their joined hands and kissed hers, then put his other hand on her cheek.

"You, grateful to me? Vivian, you have made me happier this week than I've been in years. I'm so grateful to you for that."

He leaned over to kiss her again, and they kissed for a very long time, as the fireworks exploded in front of them.

After a while, he pulled back and slowly plucked all of the pins out of her hair. She was certain her hair looked like a tangled mess now, but the way he ran his fingers through her hair made her not even care. She lifted her face up to him, and they kissed more, until he slowly pushed her back so she was underneath him on the couch.

"You are just extraordinary," he said. Good Lord, she would never get over the way he said "extraordinary" in that accent. And he was saying it about her!

She put her hand on his cheek, and they looked each other in the eyes for a very long time. Finally, he bent down and kissed her again.

"Mmm, is this the way people say thank you in England?" she asked as he pushed her dress up to her waist.

He looked up at her and grinned.

"The good ones do. Is that okay with you?"

She lifted her hands.

"Who am I to refuse to participate in a local custom?"

He laughed as he kissed her again.

Chapter Fourteen

They had to wake up far too early on New Year's Day. Vivian's flight wasn't until noon, but what with the nightmare Heathrow always was, and the time it would take them to get there, they had to leave his place no later than nine. Vivian jumped out of bed when the alarm went off and finished tucking everything into her suitcase, while Malcolm lay in bed and watched her. The night before, he'd pretended he wasn't hurt when she'd said no to his suggestion that they keep seeing each other, and now he winced when he thought about her rejection. He understood why she'd said no, he supposed, but it still stung.

And he hated that this was going to be the last time he saw her.

He got out of bed and pulled her into his arms. She nestled her head into his chest, and they stayed there like that for a long time, not kissing, not moving toward the bed or anything else, just holding each other. Finally, he pulled away and kissed the top of her head.

"I'm going to make us some coffee while you finish getting ready."

He pulled pajama pants on and went off to the kitchen. He'd bought some pastries yesterday to have this morning, so he put them in the oven to warm up while the coffee brewed. He listened to Vivian in the shower and smiled at the gasp she always made when the water came on. After not that much time, she came into the kitchen and sat at the table.

"I think I have everything," she said.

He poured her a cup of coffee and added cream and sugar to it.

"Do you have food? You need food." He set her coffee in front of her, along with the plate of pastries. "There's some leftovers from last night. I'll pack them up for you."

She smiled at him.

"Thank you."

They were both quiet over their coffee. Finally, she looked over at the clock in the kitchen.

"Malcolm, I think we should probably . . ."

He got up and nodded.

"You're right. Let me throw clothes on."

He picked up the packet of food he'd made and handed it to her.

"I hope you have room for this in your purse."

She smiled.

"If not, I'll make room."

All too soon, they were on the road to Heathrow, her luggage in the boot of his car.

He was strangely disappointed there wasn't more traffic that day. Of course there wasn't; it was the morning of New Year's Day, and everyone was recovering from the night before. But it meant they got to Heathrow faster than he'd anticipated.

He cleared his throat as they approached her terminal.

"This week was lovely, Vivian. Thank you for spending it with me." That sounded so formal, and didn't at all express how he felt, but he supposed it was better than nothing.

He could feel her eyes on him.

"I had a wonderful time. I'm so glad we did this," she said.

She put her hand on top of his. He looked over to see her smiling at him, and he smiled back. He knew she knew what he really meant, that no matter how formal he sounded, he'd loved the time he'd talked to her and laughed with her and played with her more than any few days he'd had in years.

"Let me know if your flight gets delayed, all right? Or anything like that?"

She nodded.

"I will."

They pulled up at the curb, then it was the frantic rush to pull her bags out of the boot and get her on her way. He wished he'd spent more time saying good-bye to her in the car. He felt cheated that he only had seconds to do so.

He bent down and kissed her for as long as he dared.

"Good-bye, Vivian," he said against her ear. "I'll miss you."

She looked up at him, her eyes full of tears. He hadn't expected that. He wanted to pull her close, to wipe the tears from her eyes, to tell her he'd see her next month. But he couldn't do any of that.

"Good-bye, Malcolm," she said. She took a step back, slung her purse over her shoulder, and took hold of the handle of her luggage. "Take care."

She turned and walked into the terminal, and he watched her until she was swallowed up into a sea of other travelers.

As he drove back into the city, he tried to take his mind off Vivian, and to think of things he had to look forward to. This month was a slow one for work, with the Queen still at San-dringham until early February, which had meant he'd spent a lot of time with his nephew in the past few Januarys. They'd gone on weekend adventure trips—one year Paris, another Barcelona, last year Berlin; he'd forgotten about that, with everything else going on, and Miles hadn't reminded him.

Was Vivian right about Miles?

He sighed. Of course she was right; that wasn't the question. The question was whether he was too pigheaded to apologize.

Before he even realized what he was doing, he was on his way toward his sister's house. Miles probably wouldn't even be home. He was likely off somewhere with his friends; he didn't need his uncle. He should text him instead of just showing up like this. But no matter what Malcolm told himself, he didn't change course.

When he pulled up outside of Sarah's house, he took out his phone.

> Are you at your mom's? I'm in the
> neighborhood. Can we talk?

He pressed send, then shook his head. That wasn't good enough.

> I'm sorry about how I acted on Christmas Day.
> I'd love to talk to you about your plans again. I
> promise I'll listen.

He decided he'd wait for two minutes, no more, to see if Miles would respond, then he'd drive away.

No, that wasn't enough time. Ten minutes. He could wait ten minutes.

But his phone buzzed almost immediately.

> Ok. How close are you? I'm just waking up.

Malcolm shut off his car.

> By the time you get out of the shower, I'll be
> outside.

He sent a silent thanks to Vivian.

Wait, why did it have to be silent? He wanted to be able to thank her for real. Should he text her?

He shook his head. This might make her think he was pushing for a booty call, as she had put it. She hadn't seemed exactly offended by that, but she hadn't seemed thrilled, either.

But he wanted to find a way to let her know he'd listened to her advice, and that it had helped.

Vivian unlocked her front door and dropped her umbrella in the basket in her entryway. She'd been home from England now for a full week, and it had rained almost every day. She knew she was supposed to be grateful for the rain; California was in a perpetual state of drought, after all, and her garden would be better for it, blah blah blah. She couldn't muster up any gratitude, though. She just felt as gray and depressed and lonely as the outside world looked.

She kicked off her shoes, dropped her stack of mail on her kitchen counter, and poured herself a glass of red wine.

Maybe if it stopped raining, it would get her out of this funk she'd been in ever since she'd gotten back from England. Maddie had picked her up from the airport when she'd gotten home, and she'd cheerfully told her all—well, *most*—of the things she and Malcolm had done in their days together in London, and had managed to laugh at Maddie's questions about if they were going to see each other again. But she'd barely even pretended to laugh since then.

She wasn't in denial; she knew why she was in such a funk. She'd spent five almost perfect days with Malcolm—ten, if you counted their time together at Sandringham—and she'd fallen deep into infatuation with him, and now it was all over. She was angry at herself for how ridiculous she was being— really, Vivian? Moping around because of a man? Come on.

It also didn't help to be back at work, because every day made her mourn the impending end of her current job. Yes, as the director, she would have so much more authority, and a good bump in salary, but she wouldn't get the daily interaction with patients that she treasured. There were hard days; days when she drove home full of unshed tears for how difficult some people's lives were, days when she wished so much she could have helped more, days when she was so frustrated with other people she wanted to scream. But even on days like that, she was grateful she'd been able to help a little bit, glad she'd been able to improve someone's life with her advice or her knowledge or just her presence. She knew there were lots of other great social workers who would be able to take her place; the patients would be okay. But would she?

She sipped her wine and looked at her phone. Jo had called just as she was leaving the office; she needed to call her back. But she didn't feel up to chatting with Jo right now and pretending she felt fine. Maybe she'd call her back in the morning on her way to work.

She thumbed through her stack of mail: what looked like

some belated Christmas cards, some envelopes from charities she'd supported, probably asking for more money, a postcard that was probably junk mail. Nothing interesting, in other words.

She took the mail over to her couch with her anyway. She read through the Christmas letter from someone she'd worked with years ago—far too much detail, but then, she read the whole thing, didn't she? She looked at the Christmas card from the daughter of one of her old friends and cooed over the pictures of their new baby. And she picked up that postcard to see what it was about.

Wait. The picture on the front of this postcard was that tiny sapphire and diamond tiara from the V&A.

Her hands trembled as she flipped it over.

Vivian—How's sunny California? I must thank you for your advice about how to talk to Miles—on the very day you left, I apologized to him and asked him if we could talk, and he agreed. It hasn't been perfect, but at least it's been a dialogue. He liked you very much, by the way, but then, how could anyone not?

Regards,
Malcolm

P.S. Your luggage tag with your address on it fell off your suitcase; I found it on my bedroom floor yesterday. I hope it's okay that I wrote?

He'd scrawled his address on the bottom.

She felt the smile spread across her face. She could hear his voice as she read the postcard. She'd missed him so much.

But she'd told him they shouldn't see each other anymore after she left England, and she knew she'd been right about that. If she replied to this postcard, wouldn't it just prolong her case of the winter blues?

Oh, the hell with it. She needed something to look forward to, and the sun hadn't come out in a week.

At lunchtime the next day, she went to a nearby bookstore and bought a postcard of a cable car.

Malcolm—It's rained constantly since I got home; "sunny California" indeed. I'm thrilled to hear that about you and Miles; please tell him I said hello. Has he changed his mind at all . . . or have you? Did I tell you Julia gave me her recipe for scones before I left Sandringham? I haven't tried my hand at them, but I'm going to do it as soon as I get a kitchen scale—all of her measurements are in grams!

Vivian

His next postcard came a week later. This time it had the London Eye on the front, with fireworks above it. Were those some of the same fireworks they'd seen? She laughed at herself. No, of course not; that photo had probably been taken years before. She flipped the card over.

Vivian—Neither of us has changed our minds, at least not yet, but we seem to understand what's in each other's minds a bit better. We're going fishing this weekend, which I hope will give us some time to sort things out more. And I'm agog that Julia gave you her secret scone recipe; you'll have to tell me how they turn out. Too bad we won't be able to share them. How are you feeling about that new job?

Malcolm

She grinned at the card and smiled out into her damp garden.

After that, it was rare for a few days to pass without her getting a postcard from Malcolm, or sending one to him. Every time she got home and grabbed her stack of mail out of her mailbox, she got a rush, knowing there might be a card somewhere in the pile. Whenever she walked by a bookstore or stationery store, she dipped inside to find a postcard to add to her stack at home.

She knew this was dangerous. She knew it would only prolong her feelings for Malcolm, which needed to die down already. But somehow, she couldn't bring herself to care. It was winter, the Bay Area was apparently getting three years of rain this month, and she needed something to cheer her up, something to look forward to. She would make herself worry about this in the spring.

On a Sunday afternoon, she was just getting home from the grocery store when her phone rang.

"Oh, my mother is answering the phone finally, hmm?" Maddie said.

Vivian laughed.

"Hey, girl, how's your weekend been?"

She could hear Maddie washing her dishes in the background.

"Good, except I haven't heard from you for days. Where have you been?"

Vivian opened her refrigerator to unload her groceries.

"Just working. There have been a lot of meetings in the past few days, since I become acting director in a few weeks. And yesterday I was at Aunt Jo's all day."

"Ooh, acting director so soon! When do you become permanent director?" Maddie asked.

Maddie sounded so excited and proud of her.

"They posted the job listing on Friday, so I have a month or so to put together my application."

At least four people had come by her office on Friday afternoon to make sure she knew the application was up on the hospital website. She hadn't even looked at it yet—she'd made a ton of calls on Friday to help connect a patient with services, and she'd been busy all day Saturday. She had plenty of time, though; she didn't have to look at it yet.

"Oh!" Maddie turned off the water. "Perfect timing! Have you started working on your application? Do you need any help with it? I'm sure Theo could look it over for you; he's great at that kind of stuff." Vivian heard a rumbling in the background. "See, he says he'd be happy to."

Vivian closed her refrigerator door.

"Thanks. I might take him up on that."

Maddie was silent for a moment.

"Mom, is everything okay? You sound . . . I don't know, off somehow. Is Aunt Jo okay? Is anyone else in the family sick, or . . . ?"

Vivian sat down on the couch.

"No, no, everything is fine. Aunt Jo is great, actually; I just talked to her at lunchtime. I'm just tired, I guess. Maybe I should go to bed early."

Vivian stared out the window after she got off the phone with Maddie. The rain was starting again. She sighed and got up to put away her canned goods.

Chapter Fifteen

Malcolm stopped at Waterstones on the way home to see if they had any new postcards. He had plenty of them now, all in a pile in the middle of his coffee table, but he was always looking for more.

He and Vivian wrote to each other a few times a week; sometimes, he even wrote before waiting for a reply from her, and he thought she did, too. He'd told her as much as he could fit on a postcard about his conversations with Miles, she'd told him about her recent excursions to some local museums, and they both told each other funny or entertaining or frustrating stories from their daily lives. He loved her postcards; he could hear her voice in his head as he read them. It was like she was sitting there on the couch next to him, that amusement and enthusiasm and laughter all together in her voice.

But he was getting worried about her. She'd sounded blue about her new job, which seemed already to be sucking up more and more of her time and energy, when she hadn't even started yet. She'd never seemed enthusiastic about it, and Vivian was enthusiastic about everything she cared about. When she talked about her current social work job, her love for it shone through in her words, her expressions, her very body language. None of that came through when they discussed the director position. He wished he'd said something to her about that when she was in London.

He'd felt like it wasn't his place to say that, though. They'd never really discussed finances—he knew she wasn't wealthy, and that she'd struggled to raise Maddie alone, but he had no idea if she was in a difficult spot now and really needed the money from the new job or not, and he would never ask. Maybe that's what was driving her to take this job? Because it certainly didn't seem like it could be anything else.

Was he reading her wrong? Maybe. He hadn't known her very long, after all. But he didn't think so.

He wished he could see her again. The postcards brought him joy every day, but he wanted to talk to her, hear her laughter, see her smile, evaluate the tone of her voice when she talked about this job, maybe even try to ask a few more pointed questions about it. Just to see if she'd be okay. He'd even gotten to the point of looking to see what the airfare was from London to San Francisco—very reasonable, this time of year—but had stopped himself before he'd gone any further down that road. She'd made it clear when they'd talked about this on New Year's Eve that she didn't want that.

He walked into his building and went straight for his mailbox, but he didn't look through his stack of mail until he'd walked into his flat. He didn't want to rush through her note, if it was there, or have to hold in his disappointment if it wasn't.

He sat down on the couch and dropped the stack on his coffee table. There it was. A wide, empty beach on the front. What a way to lord the whole California thing over him.

Malcolm—I was in a meeting the other day for the new job—I become acting director soon—and someone had brought something they called scones to the meeting. I spent the whole boring meeting thinking about how horrified both you and Julia would be at those terrible, rocklike scones. At least it gave me something to do instead of telling all of those people to stop listening to themselves talk and just get on with it. I should have learned more from you about how to keep a straight face at times like this; there are going to be a lot of meetings in my future.

Vivian

He had to say something. If he were Vivian, she would say something to him about this, wouldn't she? He smiled at the thought. She absolutely would.

He plucked a postcard off the top of his waiting stack and started scribbling.

V—Do you really want this job? Feel free to tell me to shut up and stop prying if you want to. I know this isn't any of my business. But I hear the difference in you when you talk about this job, versus the way you talk about your current job. I heard it when you were in England, and I can hear it even in a few lines in a postcard. I'm sure there are many reasons you think you should take it, but will it make you happy?

M

He tore off a stamp from the book in his drawer and ran outside to drop the card into the postbox before he could change his mind. Then he sat on his couch and stared out the window for a very long time.

Vivian sat at her desk at work and looked down at Malcolm's postcard in her hand. She'd been carrying it around for days now. He'd asked her a question she'd never stopped to ask herself. Would this job make her happy?

He'd asked that question so easily: "Will it make you happy?" Had he realized he'd thrown her entire worldview into chaos?

That wasn't a question she usually asked herself. In all of

her pro/con lists about her life decisions—especially when it came to jobs—that wasn't a question she ever bothered to answer. Would it improve Maddie's life, would it make her more money, would it make it easier for her to help her family, would it make other people satisfied, would it make her family criticize her, would it make her doctor approve of her? Those were all of the questions she usually asked herself.

But her own happiness? What a strange, foreign, confusing thing to think about.

"Will it make you happy?"

Her first response to that question was, "What does that matter?" She laughed at herself for that—she was a mental health professional, and she didn't think her own happiness mattered? But that was all too true.

She glanced over into her open desk drawer. Right there in the front was the hefty gift card for a local spa her coworkers had given her for her fiftieth birthday. It was four years later, and the gift card was still sitting there unused. It wasn't that she hadn't wanted to go to the spa; she had, and she'd been thrilled by the gift. She just hadn't found the time where she felt she could do something like that, just for herself.

Would this new job make her happy?

Why did that question scare her so much? It seemed selfish even to consider it. Her new job was a promotion; it would make her more money, she'd never in her life turned down anything offering her more money, and her happiness wasn't relevant when it came to work. Yes, she loved her current job, but that was a side benefit. Wasn't it?

She shook her head. She felt guilty even letting herself think about this. It was an honor, it was a promotion, it was a significant salary bump—a woman like her couldn't turn that down. Malcolm obviously didn't know her as well as he thought he did.

Maybe she should go on a walk at lunchtime, rain or no rain. She'd told enough people that getting outside could clear your head; she needed to practice what she preached.

"Vivian!"

She turned quickly and saw her boss standing in her doorway.

"Where were you? I called your name a few times," he said with a smile on his face.

She shook her head.

"Sorry, just thinking about a tricky case," she said.

He chuckled.

"That's one of the things that makes you so good at this: your dedication to your clients. But a break will help; it always does with me. Come on, it's time for that meeting with the county."

Oh. Right. She couldn't take a walk at lunchtime; she and her boss were going to another meeting together. She'd forgotten all about that, even though the whole reason she was in this dress today was because it was her "going to a meeting" dress. If she decided to take this job, Maddie had better find her a bunch more dresses like it.

"I was just thinking that I needed a break, actually," she said. She stood up and picked up her coat and umbrella.

She'd been to a handful of these meetings before when

she'd filled in for her boss, and she had always found them boring but mostly fine. She regularly ran into people she knew at them, which was fun, at least. The same was true today; she saw an old friend from graduate school, and a former colleague, both of whom she'd liked a lot. When they went around the table for introductions at the beginning of the meeting, her boss told everyone this was his last meeting and introduced her as the interim head, with a big wink, and she smiled at everyone around the table.

But then when the initial greetings ended and the Power-Point began, it hit her: this was going to be her new life. Instead of spending her days walking around the hospital and talking to patients and solving disputes, she'd be going to meeting after meeting just like this one. She'd be staring up at PowerPoint presentations and chuckling at bad jokes and discussing data and categorizing people by their diagnoses. And while all of that was important and necessary—except for maybe the bad jokes—would any of it make her happy?

Her current job made her happy. She loved joking with teenagers and helping them work with their parents, she got a burst of joy every time she helped patients advocate for themselves in the maze that was their health care, she'd cried happy tears when parents who she'd helped counsel through their babies' time in the NICU came back to show her their fat-cheeked, giggling, healthy babies. Yes, it was hard, almost every day. Yes, she needed to take more breaks from it, for her own mental health. But it also made her happy all the time.

Could she give up that happiness? For lots of meetings like

this, less time for herself, and more money? What if that money could help her travel more, or get a better car so she could go on more road trips, or buy more books? Would she have the time to do any of those things? Would she *take* the time to do any of those things? Would the job be worth it?

That night, she called Maddie.

"Hey, Mom! I'm so tired of all of this rain."

Vivian laughed.

"You and me both, girl. I keep daydreaming about sunshine."

"How was work today? Are you the boss yet?"

She cleared her throat.

"That's what I was calling to talk to you about. I become acting director next week, but . . . I'm not so sure I'm going to apply for the job."

She heard Maddie's big intake of breath, so she started talking again quickly.

"I'm not saying this because I don't think I'd be great at the job; I know I would be. And it's not because I have impostor syndrome or any of that other stuff. It's because . . . I like my job now. I *love* my job now, actually. Do I want to give that up, just for more status, and more money, and to be an example for other people? Part of the reason I wanted to do this was to help young social workers of color see they could succeed, but can't I do that just as well by mentoring the ones I work with? The job means more money, but it's also a lot more time. Will the extra money make me happy?"

She hadn't realized she felt this strongly until all of that came bursting out to Maddie.

There was silence on the other end of the line for a while.

"I'm so glad you're thinking about all of this, Mom," Maddie said. "I've been worried about you for a while, but you seemed so set on this job, it didn't occur to me that that was why you were so stressed."

Tears came to her eyes at the tone in Maddie's voice.

"I feel guilty saying all of this—I feel guilty even thinking it," Vivian said. "But I realized today I've dreaded starting this job ever since I first found out about it. But I felt like of course I had to take it, so I was going to. But now"—she shook her head—"I don't know what to do."

"Oh, Mom." Maddie sounded so contrite. "I didn't realize you felt like this about it. When you first told me about the job, it was right when we got to England, and I was so busy and distracted by work I didn't ask you enough questions about it. I'm so sorry I wasn't there for you."

Vivian sat down on the couch.

"No, don't feel bad. I didn't realize I felt like this about it, either. Someone said something that sort of . . . made me adjust my worldview. And I was thinking about the job today in a whole new way."

She'd been thinking about everything in a whole new way since she'd gotten that postcard from Malcolm.

How had he listened to her—and heard her—so well? About wanting to see a tiara, about why she hated surprises, about the job—there he'd heard what she didn't even say.

"Well"—Maddie had her businesslike voice on—"I've known plenty of people who have turned down well-paying jobs, or quit jobs in favor of ones where they made a fraction of that salary, and it was always because they wanted more balance in their life that the job with more money wouldn't give them. And, if you're having any issue with money, I can always pitch in. You know that, right? No matter what."

Tears rolled down Vivian's cheeks.

"Oh, girl, thank you, I know that," she said. "But it's not that; I'm doing just fine. More than fine, actually. But what if . . . I don't know, there are so many what-ifs. What if I get sick like Aunt Jo? I have excellent insurance, but there's so much insurance doesn't cover, and I don't want to be a burden on you. What if, I don't know, my house burns down? Or . . ."

Maddie cut her off.

"Enough with the what-ifs, Mom. You have to live for to-day, for now, not what you might think could possibly happen, years down the road. This job . . . if you take it, you'll probably stay in it until you retire, right?"

Vivian took a deep breath.

"Yeah, I probably would." She thought about that. The rest of her working life, in that job. A job that wouldn't make her happy. She'd known that, as soon as Malcolm had asked her the question.

"Don't you always tell me that life is too short to do some-thing you hate?"

Vivian laughed.

"Don't throw my words back at me! And I won't *hate* the job, it's not that, it's just . . ."

"I know," Maddie said. "I'm not going to tell you what to do, but I'll support you in whatever you decide to do. I know you know that. But I'm really glad you're thinking about this. All I've ever wanted was for you to be happy, Mom."

Vivian wiped her face with a napkin.

"Thanks, girl."

Vivian hung up the phone and put her head in her hands. Then she stood up and went to her file cabinet. She looked through her financial records: her retirement account, her savings, what her health insurance postretirement would guarantee her. Finally, she took a deep breath.

She didn't need this money. She could *use* it, no doubt, but she would be just fine without it. She could pay her mortgage, she could keep putting money into her savings, her retirement account was healthy, thanks to that corporate secretary job she'd had years ago, and she'd have excellent health insurance for the rest of her life—which was one of the reasons she'd taken this job in the first place.

She even had enough to cover some of her what-ifs. Not all of them, of course. But at least one or two.

She would be fine without the new job. She would be *happy* without it.

She went over to the drawer where she kept all of her stationery supplies and pulled out a postcard.

Malcolm—Thank you. You made me think about myself and my own happiness more than I have in years. I love my job. It makes me happy and fulfilled in a way I don't think I truly understood until this week. I'm not going to apply for the new job. I just decided this thirty seconds ago, and I'm so happy about it. You're the first person I told.

Love,

Vivian

Chapter Sixteen

M alcolm usually got a response from Vivian to his postcards within a week, eight days at the most. At least,
that's how it had been for over a month. But this time, while
he got a postcard a few days after he'd sent his—this one with
a story about one of her neighbors and his passive-aggressive
battle against the dogs on their street that made him laugh
and laugh—he knew she'd sent that postcard before she'd received his.

He had no real idea how Vivian would respond to what
he'd said. She'd always been so direct with him, but would
that translate into wanting him to be direct with her? Would
she be offended by him bringing up her finances? He knew he

never should have said that. But he'd been so worried about her, he hadn't been able to think clearly.

He'd spent too much time talking to Miles; this was the problem. They'd hashed and rehashed out his whole "we have to follow our passions" justification for dumping Oxford, and it seemed like the boy had somehow convinced him of the importance of all that. Only partly, though—he'd also convinced Miles to wait to make a final decision until he'd made another visit to Oxford and talked to his tutors again. Luckily, he'd remembered how excited Miles had been when they'd been to Oxford together, so he thought there still might be a chance.

He shrugged. And, if all failed, Miles could always apply again. Oxford would always be there. And Miles's high grades and impressive A levels would be there, too.

Finally, as he rifled through the mail in the elevator—he no longer had the self-control to wait until he got into his flat—he found a postcard with a picture of a waterfall on the front. He turned it over and read it as soon as he walked into his flat.

She wasn't going to take the job. And she'd told him first.

He read the card over twice more. Not only was she not angry at him, she was grateful to him. She'd thought about what he'd said, and it had made a difference to her.

He leaned against his door and smiled. Joy, relief, and affection for Vivian spread through him. He was so pleased she wasn't going to take the new job. And he was so happy his words had made her rethink something so important to her.

He wanted to send her a gift to celebrate this decision. Something momentous, something worthy of Vivian.

He remembered something he'd seen the week before and had talked himself out of buying. He knew just the thing.

Vivian drove up to her house and smiled at the bouquet of yellow and orange and pink flowers in the passenger seat of her car. Their bright colors had cheered her up immediately when she'd seen them in the grocery store, and she'd bought them on an impulse. Why didn't she ever buy flowers for herself? Just looking at them made her feel content and helped reassure her that no matter how much it rained, spring would come.

It hadn't been the best week at work—her boss had been hurt and angry when she'd told him she wasn't going to apply for the job, even though she'd told him she'd be happy to stay in the interim job for however long it took to hire someone else. She'd been more or less prepared for him to be upset, but she hadn't expected so many of her coworkers to stop by her office to try to get her to reconsider. But she knew she wouldn't—as soon as she'd sent Malcolm that postcard, she'd felt as if a load had been lifted off of her shoulders. The next day, she'd been happy as she walked into work for the first time in over a month. Despite everyone at work trying to change her mind, and despite how guilty and selfish she still felt, she knew she'd made the right decision.

And that very day, she'd called the spa to make an appointment to use her gift card.

She pulled a stack of catalogs out of her mailbox when she got home and sighed. Both Maddie and Jo had been happy for her—the three of them had celebrated together the day she'd given her boss the news—but she'd been waiting to hear back from Malcolm. It seemed like she wouldn't hear from him again today.

But when she dropped the catalogs on her coffee table, a postcard with a castle on the front skidded across the table. She snatched it up.

V—Congratulations! I know this must have been a very hard decision on your part, and I'm thrilled for you. I've never met a person so full of joy and warmth as you are. It makes me happy to know you'll keep stoking the fires of that joy. I'm so glad I could play even a tiny part in this decision. I hope you're drinking champagne right now. I wish I was drinking it with you.

M

P.S. Watch the post for something else to help you celebrate.

A glow spread across her whole body. He'd never met a person so full of joy and warmth? He was thrilled for her? She grinned. Yes, thank you, he *should* be thrilled for her! Everyone should be thrilled for her! She was tired of others trying to make her feel guilty! For once in her life, she'd decided to prioritize herself and her happiness; not her family's or her ex-husband's or her daughter's or her job's, but her own.

She looked for just the right postcard from her stack and sat down to write him back.

M—Thank you! I'm so glad you're thrilled for me. It really helps. People keep acting like I made this decision on a whim, but I think this was one of those decisions it took my whole life to realize. Shamefully, I don't even have any champagne in my house, but I should remedy that ASAP.

V

Her eyes landed on his postscript. What in the world could that mean? "Watch the post" could mean anything: A pile of postcards? A letter? A present? She smiled. She could hardly wait to find out.

She didn't have to wait long. Two days later, she walked up to her front porch just as a deliveryman left a note on the door.

"Is that for me?" she asked him.

"It is if you're Vivian Forest," he said. "Sign here."

She signed, then grabbed the package and opened her front door. She told herself not to get too excited—it could just be something she'd ordered online and forgotten about. But when she glanced at the postmark and saw it was from London, she let all pretense fall away and used her keys to slit open the package in a hurry.

The note was the first thing to fall out of the box.

Vivian—Congratulations again on your decision; I'm so happy for you, and glad I could play a small role in it. I'm sorry I couldn't break into the V&A and get you the real one; maybe next time. On a serious note: you are a treasure, and I hope this helps you celebrate yourself. I love the joy you find in the world.

Malcolm

What could he have sent her? She took a bubble-wrapped object out of the box, and pulled off the layers of bubble wrap. Then she gasped.

It was the tiara. Obviously not the real one, but a delightful little replica of that tiny sapphire and diamond tiara.

She put it on top of her head, looked in the mirror, and laughed out loud. She loved it so much. She felt very silly, though—wasn't she a little too old to be dressing up like a princess? She grinned at herself in the mirror again and shook that off. Who cared how old she was?

She pulled out her phone and immediately took a selfie. She scrolled through her phone to Malcolm's name, then hesitated. They hadn't texted each other since she'd gotten back—all of their contact since she'd waved good-bye on January 1 had been strictly via postcard. Should she open that back up now?

She looked back at the selfie. She looked *really* good in that tiara. It would be a shame not to share it.

And with one click, there it went, whizzing across the continents to him.

A half second after she sent it, she realized it was the middle of the night in London. Oh well, hopefully her fabulous picture either wouldn't wake him up or would give him sweet dreams if it did!

Just then, there was a knock at her door.

"Hey, Mom, it's me!"

Oh, that's right, Maddie was bringing her a dress for her great-nephew's christening. She paused on the way to the door. Should she take the tiara off before Maddie came in? Hell no—no one would share her enjoyment about this as much as her daughter would. She ran to the door and opened it.

Maddie took one look at her and a grin spread across her face.

"Where did the tiara come from?"

She turned in a circle to model the tiara.

"You're going to get all . . . *you* about this, but Malcolm sent it to me. We saw the original at a museum when I was in London. I sent him a note when I decided not to apply for the job; he sent this to me so I could celebrate."

Maddie's face was triumphant.

"Mmmmmmm." She pursed her lips and her eyes danced. "Mallllcolm sent it to you, hmmmmmm?"

Vivian laughed and rolled her eyes.

"Don't Mmmmmmm me, I'm the queen of Mmmmmmm. There's nothing to Mmmmmmm about here."

Maddie shook her finger at Vivian.

"I don't think that's true! Vivian and Malcolm sitting in a tree, K-I-S-S . . ."

They were both laughing too hard for Maddie to keep singing. Finally, Vivian caught her breath.

"Stop it. We're just friends, okay?"

Maddie dropped the garment bag she was carrying onto the couch and sat down.

"No, seriously, Mom. This all seems awfully romantic to me. You send each other notes? He sent you a tiara?" Maddie looked at the flowers in the vase on her counter. "Did he get you those flowers, too?"

Vivian adjusted her tiara.

"No, I bought myself the flowers."

Maddie's eyebrows went up.

"You bought yourself flowers? That's unlike you, in a good way. Anyway, I think this guy is seriously falling for you." She stared at Vivian, all mockery gone from her face. "Are you falling for him?"

Vivian didn't let her smile flicker.

"Madeleine. I'm not a 'falling for a stranger on vacation' kind of person. You know that."

Maddie sighed.

"I know, I know. I just want you to be happy, Mom."

Vivian hugged her daughter.

"I know you do."

But when Maddie left, Vivian sat back down on the couch with a thud.

She couldn't be honest with Maddie, but she had to be honest with herself.

Yes, she was falling for him. Even though she wasn't a 'falling for a stranger on vacation' kind of person. Even though he was over five thousand miles away.

She thought of the note he'd included with the tiara and smiled to herself. Maddie didn't know the half of how romantic it had all been. But it wasn't just the tiara and the notes. It was the way he saw her, for who she was. The way he listened to her. The way he celebrated her.

Well. She was doing what made her happy now, wasn't she?

She poured herself a glass of wine and picked up a pen.

Chapter Seventeen

Malcolm pulled into his garage after a long day at work. They were in the midst of plans for Trooping the Colour in June, in addition to monitoring the daily ups and downs of Parliament, and all the other regular government business. Speaking of, a hilarious thing had happened that day in an ambassador's audience with the Queen that he dearly wanted to tell Vivian about, but it was too sensitive for a postcard.

She'd texted him that fantastic photo in her tiara last week in the middle of the night, and the next morning, he'd told her how fabulous she looked and how he was glad it looked like she was enjoying her gift, but she hadn't responded to that. He hadn't exactly expected her to; the two of them weren't much for texting. But the tiara picture was a special occasion; maybe his bit of gossip he couldn't share with anyone else could be one, too?

When he reached into his mailbox, he felt the corners of the postcard there and smiled. Maybe her postcard would give him another excuse—not excuse; reason, he meant—to text her.

He walked in the door of his flat and sat down on the couch.

Malcolm—Thank you for the tiara, and everything you said. Since I made one big leap of faith recently, I'm going to make another one now: I'm falling in love with you. It feels ridiculous to say that—we've only known each other for a couple of months, after all. But now you have me thinking about what makes me happy—a dangerous thing to think about!—and I realized one of the answers is you.

Vivian

He must have read that too quickly. He must have gotten it wrong. He read the postcard again and dropped it face up on the coffee table.

This was impossible. Why did she tell him this? What did she expect him to do with this? They lived over five thousand miles away from each other. How was he supposed to handle this?

He went into his kitchen and poured himself a finger of scotch.

She couldn't have fallen in love with him. She liked him a lot, sure; he liked her a lot, too! That's why his original idea that they visit from time to time and have a fun week of adventure and good food and excellent sex was such a good one!

Why did she have to spoil everything by bringing emotions into it?

And no matter what he felt for Vivian, he couldn't uproot his life! He was too old for that! He had a job, and a flat, and a car, and a nephew who still needed his guidance. People like him didn't just do things like "fall in love," especially not after a Christmastime holiday with a visiting American. The whole idea was ridiculous.

He dropped a magazine on top of the postcard so he wouldn't have to look at it anymore.

Two weeks later

Malcolm walked into his flat with Miles. They were having one of their old-style weekend days—they'd spent the morning playing tennis and planned to watch a football match later this afternoon. For now: lunch.

He'd stopped to check the mail on the way into the building, but there was nothing from Vivian. Every day, he hoped he'd get another postcard from her, one that said she'd been joking, she hadn't meant it, or better yet, pretended she'd never said it in the first place, and was just another one of her funny, warm, heartfelt postcards, and they could continue on like they had been. But it had all been silence.

He hated that now every time something happened throughout the day that he wanted to tell her, he had to catch himself and remember that he couldn't. He was angry at himself that life felt so stale, flat, and unprofitable without Vivian to write to and think about and plan for. He still caught himself sometimes; he'd slow down as he walked by postcard racks, searching for one he didn't already have, before he remembered.

He wished there was something he could do to make it go back to the way it was.

He sighed and dropped their sack of sandwiches and crisps on the kitchen counter.

"Beer?"

Miles flopped on the couch like he was boneless, in that way teenagers did. From looking at him, you'd think he was completely exhausted, and not like he'd beaten Malcolm in two out of three sets, and had pushed for more.

"Do you even have to ask?"

Malcolm laughed and shook his head. He didn't, as a matter of fact, even have to ask. He opened two bottles and brought them over to the living room, along with the food. And a stack of napkins.

They turned on the football match and ate while they both looked on and off at their phones, and Miles flipped through one of the magazines on the coffee table. They didn't say much, but it was a good silence.

In the past couple of months, they'd talked a lot. He'd asked Miles challenging questions, about what would happen if he failed, about what his backup plan was, about how he would support himself in the years to come. But Miles had had answers, thoughtful answers, to all of those questions. He hadn't made this decision on a whim; he'd thought a lot of these details through, he knew what the dangers were, and he was ready for them.

Malcolm's phone buzzed. He pulled it out of his pocket and shook his head at the news alert, then sighed when he clicked on it and read the whole article. Parliament couldn't just take a break on the weekends, could they? This was going to make his week much more complicated.

"What's this?"

Malcolm looked up. Miles had Vivian's postcard in his hand.

Fuck.

Malcolm reached for it, but Miles was faster than him. He jumped up and kept reading as Malcolm tried to snatch it away.

Fuck fuck fuck. Why had he left the postcard on the table in the first place? He knew why—he didn't want to pick it up and have to see it again, so he'd just left it there and covered it with more and more magazines. When did Miles decide he was so interested in reading magazines that he got to the bottom of that stack?

Miles grinned at him over the postcard.

"Go, Vivian! Brilliant, I really liked her. What did you say? You love her, too, don't you? Is she coming back soon?"

Malcolm sighed.

"No." He looked over at the book Vivian had finished while she was there and left on his end table for him to read. "No, she isn't."

Miles dropped the postcard on the table.

"No? Why not? Wait." Miles gave him that superior teenager look he hated. "What did you do? How did you manage to screw this one up? Did you even answer her?"

Malcolm glared at his nephew.

"None of this is any of your business. You shouldn't be reading my private correspondence anyway."

Miles rolled his eyes.

"Well, you shouldn't be leaving your 'private correspondence' around for the whole world to read, especially if it's on a postcard!" Miles shook his head. "I can't believe you did this to Vivian. I thought you liked her! You certainly talk about her enough."

He wanted to wipe the smirk off the little jerk's face.

"I do like her. Unfortunately, I'm an adult, not a teenager. Just liking someone—even loving someone—isn't enough to change your whole life. She lives in California, I live in London, there's no future for us. We shouldn't have gotten this entangled in the first place."

Miles sat down next to him.

"That's your only reason? Are you forgetting airplanes exist?"

Malcolm sighed.

"Miles, it's not just about the distance; that was only one example. We're just very different people, and the whole idea is impractical. It's too risky."

Miles laughed.

"Risky? What are you risking here? Ooh, is it your feelings?"

He needed to throw his nephew out of his apartment.

"I told you, this is none of your business."

Miles took another sip of beer.

"So what, then, you're just going to live the rest of your life knowing that you love her and she loves you but you're too scared to just go for it?"

"I'm not scared, and I didn't say I loved her!" Malcolm said.

Miles smirked again.

"You didn't have to."

Malcolm stood up to get another beer. And to get away from this conversation. Miles glanced in his direction, opened his mouth once or twice, but didn't say anything else.

For the next hour, Malcolm tried to concentrate on the football match, but instead he stewed about his conversation with Miles. There were plenty of reasons he hadn't responded to Vivian. He wasn't scared; he was just practical. They lived in very different places, they had very different careers, she was direct and effusive and chatty; he was the opposite of all of those things, and it would never work between them.

"You're right: it's none of my business," Miles said out of the blue. "But . . . you've said a lot lately about how I should have a baseline of success and respect from the world before following my dreams. But you have that! People respect you more than anyone I know, and instead of taking advantage of that now, it seems like the rest of your life is standing in your own way." He shrugged. "I just . . . I really liked her."

Malcolm sighed.

"Yeah. Me too."

But that was a lie. He knew it was a lot more than that. He

just had no idea what to do about it. It all seemed impossible. Too hard, too risky, too complicated. And it might be useless— what if he tried, and it didn't work out between them, and they'd both sacrificed for no reason? What if she was so angry at him for ignoring her for weeks that she'd realized he wasn't the person she thought he was?

But what if it was all worth it?

Chapter Eighteen

Vivian had never been one for wallowing. She'd always been in the "let yourself have a good cry and get it all out, then move on to the next thing" camp. At least, that's the advice she'd always given to Maddie, and to various patients and friends.

She'd tried hard to take her own advice, over these past three weeks since she'd sent that postcard to Malcolm. But the tears just wouldn't come.

They'd hovered, so close she could feel them, ever since she'd dropped that postcard in the mailbox. When she sent it, she'd hoped he'd call her as soon as he got it, time difference or no time difference, to tell her he was falling in love with her, too. She'd thought she had reason to hope; that the tiara was a symbol of how he felt for her.

But then she worried she'd read it wrong, and that he might send her a card back to say he had feelings for her, but that their lives were too different and far apart to do anything about how they felt. And of course, at three in the morning, she thought he'd say he'd had a great time with her over the holidays, but love didn't come into it, or sometimes that he'd send her a postcard and not mention her declaration at all.

She didn't, however, think he might just leave her in limbo like this. Forever.

It had taken her a while to realize that was what he was going to do. For the first week, she'd checked her phone and her mailbox obsessively. After a week had gone by, she'd gotten worried, that maybe something was wrong, that something had happened to him. But no, that was the useful thing about him being an actual public figure—she'd googled him, and everything seemed fine. Then she wondered if he'd never gotten her card at all, and that's why he hadn't responded to it. But she'd rejected that idea; he would have kept writing to her if that had been the case. No, this silence seemed pointed.

She'd thought he was better than this.

She knew she deserved better than this.

At least she was glad he'd helped her realize how much she loved her job. She was still the interim director until they hired someone permanently, but she'd gotten called in to deal with a tricky case earlier that week, one that had made her proud of the work she'd done, and happy she'd get to go back to that work full-time soon. She'd helped a family deal with the aftermath of a car accident, navigated the various services that applied to them, and repaired a few relationships between family members on the way. She didn't flatter herself that those relationships would stay repaired forever, but at least it was a step, and the whole family had seemed genuinely grateful to her for her work with them. The teenage patient had been released that day, and she hoped he'd come back to visit, in maybe a few months, or a year, and let her know how he and his family were all doing.

She knew she was doing the right thing, she knew she was in the right place, she knew she'd made the right decision about that job. This was her talent, this was her skill, this was what she loved to do.

She just wished . . .

She shook her head and turned on the radio.

Ten minutes later, she pulled into her driveway. She smiled at the flowers in her yard as she got out of her car; thank goodness spring seemed like it was finally here. When she turned to her front steps, she jumped. Why was someone sitting on her front steps?

She backed away, ready to duck inside her car and decide whether to call the police or to just wait the guy out. She usually tried to avoid calling the police, but she didn't know what to do in a situation like this. She was a social worker, sure, but—

"Vivian! It's me!"

She stopped and looked at the guy on her porch directly for the first time.

"It's me. Malcolm."

She dropped her purse to the ground.

It really was him. He had an overnight bag and a bouquet of flowers next to him. He looked rumpled and sleep-deprived and worried. And perfect.

"What are you doing here?" she asked.

"I got your postcard," he said.

She looked at him for a long moment.

"The one I sent three weeks ago? Was there some sort of nationwide mail shutdown in Britain I didn't hear about?"

He shook his head.

"I deserved that. No, there wasn't. It just took me . . . a while . . . to figure everything out."

He stood up and took a step toward her. She didn't move.

"What did you figure out, then?"

He folded his hands together, then dropped them by his sides.

"I know you hate surprises. I'm sorry, and I'll leave right now if you want me to. But I had to talk to you, and I couldn't wait for the mail, and I didn't want to do this over the phone."

If he'd come all this way for a bad surprise, she was going to create a motherfucking international incident over it.

"None of that explains why you're standing on my front porch right now," Vivian said.

He nodded.

"Right, yes, I know that. The thing is, I'm not good at this, as I think you are aware. I do this thing—I pull away, I brood about things, I shut down. You saw me do it in London . . .

more than once, actually, but you brought me out of it. Well, there was no you around after your postcard arrived, so Miles had to be the one to make me realize what a fool I'd been." He laughed. "See, there's another thing you fixed for me: I would have ruined my relationship with Miles for years if it wasn't for you getting me to pull my head out of my ass."

The tears still hovered, but she wouldn't let them come. Not yet.

"What did Miles make you realize?" she asked.

He took a step toward her.

"That I've fallen in love with you, too. And that I'm not too old, or too entrenched in my career, or too conservative to let myself fall for you. This part I figured out for myself: even though I have no real idea what we're going to do about the continent and ocean that divide us, or if I'll be able to stop being a jackass and sort out my feelings, or if we have a future together, it doesn't matter, because right here, right now, I love you. I won't blame you if you've given up on me, but I couldn't last one more day without seeing you and telling you all of this and the two of us trying to figure all of that out together."

She saw the hopeful, scared smile on his face. She took a step toward him.

"Are you sure?"

He nodded.

"So sure that I'm terrified. I'm not used to not knowing how to do things. But I love you so much that I want to try anyway."

She smiled up at him, and the tears finally fell.

"I do, too," she said.

She walked up her front steps, and he pulled her into his arms.

"This doesn't feel like real life," she said against his chest.

He kissed her hair.

"To me either. It feels too good to be real. Maybe we can try to believe in it together?"

She tilted her head back and smiled at him. He brushed the tears from her cheeks.

"I've missed you so much," he said. "I've missed your postcards, too, but . . . it's wonderful to see you in real life. To hold you." He pulled back and traced her lips with his thumb. "To kiss you."

She pulled back before he could kiss her. He tried to pull her close again, but she held up a finger.

"Hold on a second."

She went back and picked up her purse from where she'd dropped it so she could unlock her front door.

"Now you can kiss me," she said when they were safely inside. "My neighbors don't need the show!"

He laughed and pulled her into his arms.

Epilogue

Nine months later

Malcolm untangled yet another string of Vivian's Christmas lights.

"So let me get this straight. You're telling me that in America there's NO Christmas cake? None at all?"

Vivian plugged in the string he was untangling, and she smiled when all of the lights came on.

"We have Christmas cake. All kinds. Chocolate and pumpkin and cranberry, even some bûche de Noëls. There was a great spice cake one of my sisters made a few years ago."

He shook his head.

"No no no. None of that nonsense you just listed out to me is Christmas cake. Christmas cake starts months in advance; it's a dense, heavy cake, none of your fluffy, layered American nonsense. And best of all, you feed it with whiskey every week for the months leading up to Christmas. It's delicious and you get drunk while eating it; it's one of my favorite things about Christmas."

They'd spent the last nine months talking a lot, texting a lot, and sending hundreds of postcards. At least once a month, one or the other of them came for a visit—sometimes as short as a weekend, but even a few days made a difference. They'd committed early on to talking things through, even when it was hard, and to jumping in with each other, feet first.

It had all been impossibly hard, and incredibly wonderful.

Vivian grinned at him.

"If it takes months to make it, why did you tell me about this five days before Christmas? Now I want to try it."

He grinned back at her.

"I'll put it on the calendar for next year, then. We'll make one in October, for next Christmas."

Her smile got wider.

"Deal."

They were going to have more time together in this New Year. He would stay here with Vivian until late January, and in February, he would start a new job at a consulting firm— one with offices in London and San Francisco. His last day at the palace had been two days ago; he'd been sad to leave, but ready. The Duchess had somehow gotten wind of everything and had sent him a gift addressed to Ms. Vivian Forest and Mr. Malcolm Hudson.

He climbed up on Vivian's tiny ladder to put the star on top of her Christmas tree.

"How were you going to put this up here if I hadn't been here with you? This tree is huge!"

Vivian rolled her eyes at him.

"That's why I waited for you to decorate my tree, obviously." She blushed and looked down. "Well, that's one of the reasons."

He didn't think he could love her more, then she said things like that. And when he was stuck on this ladder, too. It was a good thing he'd tucked some mistletoe in his suitcase.

"You know," he said, "I've been so busy in the last few weeks with all the last-minute stuff at work, and packing to come here, that we haven't had time to talk about our January holiday." He'd convinced her to take most of the month off, but they hadn't planned any of it yet. "Where should we go?"

She smiled up at him, her face lit by hundreds of multicolored Christmas lights.

"I don't know," she said. "Surprise me."